She didn't have to explain herself to him

Why did he keep forcing her on the defensive. "This is peak holiday time. It's just a temporary phase," she went on. "By October..."

"Exactly, by October. By October you will be busy again. By October you'll have more staff available. By October, Adam will have missed his deadline. Right now you're sitting twiddling your thumbs and turning down a vacancy which fits yoou like a glove. What's the matter? Are you afraid of getting your hands dirty?"

Cathy realized she was about to lose her temper, but decided she didn't care. She wouldn't let this disturbing man bulldoze her. "Perhaps I don't see why I should go out of my way to be bullied by a loutish Yorkshireman," she flashed.

ELEANOR REES lives on the very edge of a little Chilterns town with a man who is the model for all her heroes—or so she tells him—and two cats. The cats, she says, approve of her writing as it keeps her lap stationary for long periods of time. Plus, the cats make their own contribution by strolling up and down the computer keyboard when Eleanor isn't looking. Her ambition is to write full time and to live in the sort of place that gets snowbound in the winter. "I can't think of anything more romantic," she says.

ELEANOR REES

the seal wife

Harlequin Books

TORONTO • NEW YORK • LONDON
AMSTERDAM • PARIS • SYDNEY • HAMBURG
STOCKHOLM • ATHENS • TOKYO • MILAN

Harlequin Presents first edition July 1990
ISBN 0-373-11285-8

Original hardcover edition published in 1989
by Mills & Boon Limited

CHAPTER ONE

ADAM DALE did not seduce his housekeepers. Nor did he beat them, drink their wages, or expect them to sleep in a scarcely converted, unheated hayloft. From all these points of view, he was a model employer. So why was it that not one of the three women Cathy had selected had lasted more than a month?

One never returned to the Far Corners Agency. The latest described him passionately as the most obnoxious man she had ever met. Sighing, Cathy picked up the letter, its spiky black handwriting demanding an immediate replacement. Mr Dale was one of her more difficult clients.

She turned back to the tall blonde girl sitting opposite her across the desk. 'So what happened, Helga?' she asked patiently. 'Something must have happened for you to leave so suddenly. You were doing so well, too; nearly a month.'

The girl nodded and leaned forward. 'He is hateful,' she said. 'Nothing I do is good enough, but I ignore him. I cook and clean and I ignore him. But to throw dead animals at me before breakfast—it is too much. I come home.'

Cathy was startled. In the two years since she had started the agency, she had met with a wide variety of unreasonable behaviour from her clients, but pelting the staff with furry bodies was something new. 'Dead animals, Helga? What sort of animals?' In the background, she could hear stifled giggles from her assistant, Sally.

'Oh, I do not know. Rabbits, hares, perhaps. It is not important. I am making my breakfast and he comes into the kitchen. He throws animals at me and I catch without thinking. There is blood all over my dressing-gown before I drop them. And he says I must skin and gut them before they go cold. Before my breakfast! And so many—six, seven, eight. I tell him I will not and he swears at me. So I come home. It is too much!'

Cathy was inclined to agree with her. She herself had been brought up on a farm and could face dead rabbits with comparative equanimity. But eight before breakfast... Something would have to be done about Mr Dale.

'Never mind, Helga. You did well to last so long, I think, and we've got something else that will suit you down to the ground. I was wondering who we could send. Sally will give you the details. I hope you have a good time to make up for this last one.'

Not until the tall Swedish girl had left did Cathy and Sally dissolve into laughter.

'Rabbits!' gasped Sally. 'Oh, my goodness—I thought I was going to explode. No wonder they keep leaving. Poor Helga! What did he do to the others, I wonder?'

Cathy shrugged. 'I hate to think. The first one was that Tarrant girl—you know, the debby one. She was a mistake, really, but of course I didn't know then what he was like. I haven't seen her since. When I phoned to make sure that she was all right, her mother just told me that she had enrolled on a secretarial course and wanted her name taken off the agency books. I would think one rabbit mid-afternoon would have been enough to finish her, poor girl.'

'So who did the big bad wolf eat next?'

'Mrs Ironbrand—she must have been a substantial mouthful. I sent her just in case it was sex that reared its ugly head with the Tarrant girl, but they had a big row about Dale's daughter. She runs pretty wild, apparently, so Mrs Ironbrand decided to "take her in hand"—whatever that means—but the girl objected and so did Dale. The poor woman was much too ladylike to give me the details, but I gather it was hot stuff. She didn't mention any flying corpses.'

'And then Helga?'

'Mmm. Look, what are we going to do about the man?' Catherine was suddenly serious again. 'Listen to this.' She picked up his letter again. ' "I would be grateful if you would send an applicant prepared to stay more than a few weeks, as the constant changes are upsetting my household." He's impossible.'

'Who were you thinking of sending into the firing line now?'

Cathy shook her head. 'That's the problem— there's no one suitable on the books at all at the moment. By October I could take my pick, but just now anyone with any experience is out on holiday cover or else away themselves. All that's left is a few temporaries.'

'They're no good for this,' Sally agreed. 'Dale would eat them alive. It looks to me as if you'll just have to turn him down. It's his own fault; he was lucky to get Helga. He can't expect you to provide a constant supply of human sacrifices for him to tear apart.'

Cathy sighed, and pushed the letter away. 'I suppose you're right, but I hate the idea of turning business away. It would be our first ever failure, you realise? I think I'll phone round some of the other agencies first and see if they can help.'

'We could run a special advert, perhaps. "Wanted, housekeeper for misogynist recluse with savage daughter in remote farmhouse in Yorkshire Dales. Deafness an advantage. Must be rabbit-proof."'

'At the salary he's offering, we'd probably get replies,' Cathy pointed out. 'Whatever else, he's not hard up. He's some kind of writer, I seem to remember. Perhaps he's an eccentric millionaire.'

The other girl shuddered. 'I can't imagine why anyone would live on a farm if they didn't have to.' She looked with satisfaction round the little office with its cool pastel decoration and cheerful modern furniture, then back at her friend. 'You'd go back if you could, though, wouldn't you?'

Cathy didn't answer at once. Her mind went back to the farm where she had grown up in the Devon countryside. Not a big farm, but once quite prosperous in a small way, with a herd of pedigree Jersey cattle that had been built up by her great-grandfather. Eighty years of breeding knocked down to the highest bidder at the bankruptcy sale. Farming wasn't for farmers any more, it was for businessmen. And her father had had no head for business.

'I'm not sure I would. I miss the country, but I'd hate one of these huge farms where the animals are just production units. Small farms just don't make money any more. I couldn't go back to living on a permanent overdraft.'

She shook her head to clear the nostalgic mood which threatened to overtake her, and one of the pins which held her unruly dark hair in a pleat came flipping out. 'Damn,' she said, trying unsuccessfully to stop the springy coil from unravelling. 'Sally, could you give me a hand?'

Her assistant expertly twisted her hair back into place above the collar of Cathy's businesslike grey suit and started to adjust the pins. 'I don't know why you don't wear it loose. It suits you much better.'

'I don't want it to suit me—I want to look professional. And older. Actually, I was thinking of getting a pair of glasses as well, so that I could peer at people over the top of them—then they might not realise that I'm only twenty-three. They all expect some ancient battleaxe, and I'm sure when they see me they think they've come to the wrong place.'

Sally snorted in disbelief. 'Rubbish! You know perfectly well that most of them think you're

Superwoman in disguise. There, how's that?' She stood back to admire her handiwork. 'So what are you going to do about Dale? Personally, I think we're better off without him, even if he does pay well. You've already lost one girl; suppose you'd lost Helga? With her cooking, she's worth her weight in quails' eggs.'

'I suppose you're right,' Cathy agreed uneasily. 'And anyway, if I can't find anyone I won't have any choice. But I'll do a bit of phoning round before I give up.'

But, by the end of the afternoon, she had to admit defeat. She was going to have to tell Dale that she couldn't supply a replacement, and, even though it was his own doing, the failure rankled. Far Corners specialised in difficult places—and difficult people. And she prided herself on providing the ideal applicant for each vacancy.

Her first profits had been invested in a small personal computer on which she recorded every scrap of information about staff and clients. As the business grew, it was increasingly proving its value, allowing her to match requirements down to the last detail.

But technology couldn't help with her basic problem at the moment; the agency was just too busy. There were no experienced staff available until October and, clever as the computer was, it couldn't create them. There was no point running the program—she knew what the answer would be. There was nothing for it but to compose her first admission of failure and give it to Sally to type. It was a bad end to the day.

Fortunately, in view of the agency's lack of staff, business was very slow over the next week. Helga's return, although creating one problem, had solved another, and the only outstanding vacancies were for temporary holiday cover. It was so quiet that Cathy was almost taken by surprise by the authoritative rap on the door which interrupted her solitary lunch in the office.

She pushed her sandwich into a drawer and patted her hair to check that it was still more or less intact. Then, slipping on the severe and completely useless spectacles that she had obtained from a bemused optician the day before, she stood up just as the door opened to admit a visitor who made her neat little office look like a children's Wendy-house. As he walked across the room, Cathy wanted to rush out in front of him and clear a way through the closely packed and suddenly fragile-seeming furniture.

'Good afternoon,' he said, stretching out a broad hand. 'I'm looking for a Miss C. Aylward.'

He was broad-shouldered as well as tall; lean and powerfully built. He stood between her and the light from the window and the sun licked his hair with tongues of dark gold flame. His hand was hard and dry, and enclosed hers with the casual assurance of strength. Cathy realised that she hadn't answered his greeting; he was looking at her oddly. She cleared her throat.

'Do excuse me; I was wool-gathering, I'm afraid. I am Miss Aylward. Please sit down.' She gestured towards one of the flimsy chairs and heard it creak as he lowered his tall frame on to the seat and leaned back. 'What can I do to help you?'

Seated, Cathy could see his face clearly for the first time. He looked...leonine, that was the word. A mane of tawny hair, a golden tan, green eyes. The heat of the stuffy London day had dusted his forehead with tiny beads of sweat and a few stray tendrils of hair stuck to the damp skin. His mouth— oh, no! He was speaking and she hadn't been listening to a word he said.

'...very disappointed that you can't help, so I said I would come round to see if we can come to any arrangement.'

'I—I'm sorry, but I didn't catch your name.' What was the matter with her?

He gave her another odd look. Was she imagining the faintest hint of contempt? Probably not; he must think she was half-witted. She must snap out of this peculiar mood.

His reply saw to that. 'I'm Nicholas Ballantyne.'

The name hovered between them for a moment before Cathy placed it. 'Not Nicholas Ballantyne the novelist?'

He smiled. 'It depends whether or not you believe my critics. But yes, that Nick Ballantyne. Which indirectly is why I'm here. I share a publisher with your client, Adam Dale. He told me that you had refused to send him a replacement housekeeper and asked me if I could drop by and see if I could help smooth things over.'

'Oh, I'm sorry. Mr Dale must have misunderstood my letter. It wasn't that I refused to send someone; I simply didn't have anyone suitable. This is the worst time of year for staff, especially at short notice. And he really has only himself to blame for the previous girl leaving.'

Her visitor lounged back in the insubstantial chair until Cathy felt quite alarmed for it. 'Well, I promised Adam I would call in,' he said lazily. 'But frankly, now that I'm here, I can see that it has all been a misunderstanding. You see, Adam was under the impression that this was a specialist agency.'

'We are a specialist agency.' Cathy felt herself on the defensive. 'We specialise in out-of-the-way locations and difficult situations. There is no misunderstanding there. But unfortunately, at the moment——'

'Oh, come on. Those women you sent Adam were hardly specialists, surely? One debutante whose experience of country life was gleaned from weekend house-parties in stately homes——'

'Well, yes, she was a mistake, looking back, but——'

'One frustrated nanny who seemed to forget that she had been engaged as a housekeeper.'

'That's hardly fair! She was only trying——'

'—and one Swedish fashion-plate who thinks meat grows in little polystyrene trays on supermarket shelves. Not what I would call specialists in rural housekeeping.'

Cathy was flustered, but fought to keep her voice even. 'Mr Ballantyne, what you fail to realise is that if your friend had gone to any other domestic agency he would have been lucky to attract even one applicant for the post, never mind three. Our staff are specialists, not because they are necessarily highly trained or experienced, although many are, but simply because they are prepared to consider working in the middle of nowhere, for people whose social skills, shall we say, are frequently somewhat rusty. Or, as in this case, non-existent.'

She felt the anger rise in her and stopped, breathless, before she could betray it in her voice. If he knew so much about Dale's previous housekeepers, surely he must realise that the man was impossible? It was so unfair...

As if he had read her thought, Ballantyne went on, 'I think you are being unfair, Miss Aylward. I've no doubt that Adam behaved badly, but try to see his point of view. He's extremely busy at the moment, with a book due at the publishers at the end of next month and a thirteen-year-old daughter home from school. He really can't manage without a housekeeper. A competent housekeeper, used to country life, who can cope with the sort of work that that entails. He goes to an agency which claims to specialise in exactly that sort of post and they send a string of idiotic women——'

'Mr Ballantyne!'

'Of urban women, then, who leave in hysterics when their incompetence drives him to lose his temper. He made it clear in his original letter what he needed. It would have been more honest to admit then that the "Far Corners" in which your agency operates are nearer to Richmond Park than Richmond, Yorkshire.'

Cathy took a deep breath and tried again. 'Look, I have explained our position. If we restricted our books to farmers' wives or daughters we would have turned away dozens of satisfied clients. I'm sorry we couldn't find anyone for this position, but I doubt very much if your friend would have done better elsewhere. In fact, I phoned round the other agencies on his behalf before writing back, and there was nothing. Perhaps he should try advertising locally—or is he afraid that they'll know what he's like?'

She glared across the desk and the stranger stared coolly back. Cathy felt the back of her neck begin to prickle under his scrutiny. To break the tension, she smiled and said, 'Even the benefits of modern technology don't extend to creating housekeepers out of electronic impulses, I'm afraid.'

Ballantyne seemed to notice the grey boxlike shape and screen of the computer for the first time. 'An executive toy?' he queried contemptuously.

'Not at all!' Cathy rushed indignantly to its defence. 'The bigger the agency gets—and we're growing all the time—the more useful it is. It does more work here than I do.'

'So what does it do, then, this magic box of yours?' He stood up and walked round to behind Cathy's chair, peering over her head at the screen. She could feel his breath gently stirring her hair.

Hurriedly, she started to explain. 'It's just like a card-index file, really, with cards for all my employees and my customers. But the advantage is that if I want to find a particular reference, I don't have to search through by hand. The computer does it for me, in a matter of seconds. I can match staff to clients—when I've got any staff—like a dating agency matches potential lovers.'

His warm breath ruffled her hair again as he bent nearer. 'Show me,' he said.

Was he deliberately trying to make her uncomfortable? One large hand was planted on the desk on either side as he loomed over her. If she leant back, her back would touch his chest. Cathy shuddered involuntarily and concentrated on her program.

'Look, these are all the basic categories you can choose from. Things like cooking, car driving, non-smoker, fond of children, likes animals—all sorts of things that people like to specify when they come to me for staff. I just go down the screen and pick out the ones that are important for a particular job.'

She had caught his interest, it seemed. The veiled hostility, that slight edge of contempt, had disappeared from his voice and he sounded quite friendly. 'Can you run the program to demonstrate? Pretend I'm a client.'

'OK, then, we'll take this housekeeping job. Male or female?'

'Female.'

'Just as well, as I don't have any male housekeepers on the books. But if I did, you'd get the choice. So... cooking ability—five, I think. That's about half-way—a good, plain cook. A chef would be ten. Car driver?'

'Yes.'

'Right. Non-smoker, yes. Farm experience, definitely.' Cathy ran down the rest of the options, picking and choosing, then pressed a button and the display changed.

'There, you are—that's what you want. A female, non-smoking, plain-cooking housekeeper with farm experience, and so on. Now, if you like, I can arrange them in order of importance so if you didn't much mind about the cooking, I could put that last. You see?'

'Can I ask for a pretty one?'

Cathy flushed. 'Well, actually, yes, but I don't offer people that choice. It's more often the other way around. Quite a lot of wives insist on plain staff—if I sent Helga, they'd just find some excuse to send her back. Sometimes, if it's an invalid, I specify a pretty face to cheer them up. Look.' She typed a few words and a new line appeared on the screen.

'I want her to be beautiful.'

'That's ten then, but don't hold out too much hope. We don't have many tens.' She entered the figures and pressed another button. 'I'd normally put the starting date in now, so it would ignore anyone who isn't available. It knows holiday dates for all our current staff, and which people only work in the summer, or during school terms or whatever. But as this isn't real, I'll leave the date out. So now all we have to do is let it search the files.'

'For my perfect woman.'

'Your perfect housekeeper, yes. But I doubt if it will find her. You've been too particular.'

'What happens then?'

'If it can't find a complete match, it starts looking for one that meets most of the requirements and prints it out with a note that some of the features don't fit. That's what usually happens; few people get exactly what they would like.'

The computer made a beeping sound and paper started to feed out of the printer. Ballantyne tore it off.

'There she is, you see; your ideal housekeeper— or the nearest we can supply. Who is it?' asked Cathy.

'Catherine Aylward.'

Cathy snatched the sheet of paper and stared at it uncomprehendingly. 'It can't be, I'm not even on the file.' It was as if the computer had suddenly taken on a life of its own and decided to play a practical joke. Then it dawned on her what had happened.

'Of course!' she laughed. 'When I first bought the computer, I put all my own details in first to experiment and I've never got round to clearing them off. I'd forgotten about it. The computer would normally ignore them, you see, because I'm down as never being available for work—it's just because we didn't specify any particular date that it has picked me up.'

He took the print-out back and ran his eye down the details. 'A perfect match,' he said mockingly. 'Right down to the ten for outstanding beauty. I think the computer must have seen you without those ridiculous glasses.'

Cathy blushed furiously. She had forgotten about that. 'It was just an experiment. It wasn't real. I just put down anything.'

'But the rest of it, the farm experience and so on, that's real, is it?'

'Oh, yes—I've lived most of my life on a farm.' Then she realised where his remarks were heading. 'But I'm not going to Yorkshire, if that's what you're getting at. I run this agency; I don't work for it.'

Ballantyne walked slowly back round the desk and sat down. 'Yes,' he said after a pause. 'I can see that an agency like this must take a lot of running. Someone has to compose all the letters telling people that you have no staff available; I can see that.'

'This is peak holiday time.' Why did he keep forcing her on to the defensive like this? She didn't have to explain herself to him. 'Naturally it's a slack period. Normally I'm rushed off my feet.' Or was, before I took Sally on, she thought ruefully. There had been too much work for one person—but there was nowhere near enough to keep two busy. Something would have to be done...

'It's just a temporary phase,' she went on, dragging her mind back to the immediate problem. 'By October...'

'Exactly, by October. By October, you will be busy again. By October, you'll have more staff available. By October, Adam will have missed his deadline. Right now you're sitting twiddling your thumbs and turning down a vacancy which fits you like a glove. What's the matter? Are you afraid of getting your hands dirty?'

Cathy realised that she was about to lose her temper, but decided recklessly that she didn't care. She would not allow this disturbing man to bulldoze her. 'Perhaps I don't see why I should go out of my way to be bullied by a loutish Yorkshireman who specialises in misogyny,' she flashed.

'And perhaps you shouldn't pretend that your agency can cope. Nobody forced you to advertise that you specialise in "difficult situations". You've sent Adam three candidates who didn't work out because, frankly, they didn't have the experience. That left him in a very difficult situation. It's imperative that he has live-in help at least until his daughter goes back to school, and your last woman leaving couldn't have happened at a worse time. I'm not denying that there were faults on both sides, but after all, you are paid to solve problems, not create them. And Adam is willing to pay very generously if you solve his.'

'I run a domestic agency, not a psychiatric clinic——' she started sarcastically, but was interrupted by the opening of the office door. Ballantyne stood up politely as Cathy's assistant entered the room. Sally stared at the stranger in stunned admiration.

'Good afternoon,' she said meaningfully. 'So this is how Cathy spends her lunch times, is it? I wondered how she found it so easy to resist my suggestion of a hamburger.'

Cathy flushed. 'Sally Jameson, my assistant,' she introduced. 'Sally, this is Mr Nicholas Ballantyne, the novelist. He is here on behalf of our client Mr Dale, and I was trying to explain that we had no staff free at the moment.'

Ballantyne turned the full warmth of his smile on the newcomer. 'I'm very pleased to meet you, Sally. Cathy was just telling me how you could run this whole office on your own.'

She fell for it before Cathy could intervene. 'Oh, well, at the moment my hamster could run it,' she said flippantly. 'We haven't any new clients, and if we did, we wouldn't have any staff to send them. No staff and no customers—it streamlines the operation considerably.'

'Sally——' hissed Cathy warningly, but her assistant's attention was wholly concentrated on the writer's handsome, smiling face.

'So if your boss were to decide to spend a few weeks in Yorkshire—keeping in touch by phone, of course—you could cope?'

'Well...' She strung the word out doubtfully and Cathy breathed a sigh of relief. Then she went on,

'I doubt if I'd manage to finish the crossword every day without her. But otherwise I think I could cope.'

Nick turned triumphantly to Cathy, and, for the first time, Sally sensed the discord between them.

'Oh, dear, have I said the wrong thing? Cathy's the boss, you know.'

'I'm glad someone remembers that,' Catherine said grimly. 'Mr Ballantyne seems to be under the impression that *he* is. This agency is my livelihood and I have no intention of deserting it for the sake of obliging one client—particularly one who has behaved so badly to my staff. I'm sorry, Mr Ballantyne, but it is out of the question. Quite out of the question.'

CHAPTER TWO

CATHY looked down at her half-packed suitcase with a mixture of puzzlement and exasperation. How on earth had she let herself by persuaded into leaving at such short notice? Why, for that matter, had she agreed to go at all? It was extremely unlikely that her employer would show the slightest gratitude.

But then, if she was honest, it wasn't any thought of Adam Dale that had persuaded her to give in. The credit, or blame, for that lay with Nick Ballantyne, whose persuasive charm had made the plan seem like the solution to all their problems. And there was no doubt that the money would come in very useful; he had increased his, or rather Dale's, offer to more than twice the normal rate. In advance. It would pay for the next set of advertisements and cover Sally's salary for a month at least.

Cathy sighed. Somehow she was going to have to deal with the problem of her assistant, and it wouldn't make it any easier knowing that she had held the fort for a whole month while Cathy was away.

When her friend had left her previous job as secretary to a well-known firm of literary agents, after an unhappy love-affair with her married boss, Far

Corners had been going through a busy spell. Cathy had been hard pushed to cope and it had seemed almost providential that Sally was suddenly free. On impulse, she had offered her a part-time job and the other girl had accepted at once. It had seemed like an ideal arrangement.

Now, Cathy realised that she had been wrong. Looked at in a businesslike fashion, the agency just couldn't afford a second employee, even part-time. As a one-woman business it had flourished, in a modest way. Now, a bad few months could finish them. But how could she sack her best friend?

Well, at least now she had time to think what to do. She would have to suggest that she start looking around for another job. Sally had plenty of contacts in the publishing world—although she had been adamant that she never wanted to risk meeting her ex-lover again. But the scars had been fresh then; perhaps now she wouldn't mind so much. She had certainly been chattering away to Ballantyne happily enough that afternoon, finding friends and acquaintances in common and exchanging the latest gossip.

Cathy glanced at her watch. Half-past nine already—the packing would have to wait. If she didn't phone her mother now, she would have gone to bed. She dialled the number and listened to the long series of clicks as the call was transferred to the far north of Scotland.

Her mother's voice came over with surprising clarity, and Cathy smiled at the picture it conjured up. 'Good evening, this is Mr Balfour's residence.

Can I help you?' Her manner had all the dignity of a Victorian parlourmaid and her daughter suspected that it had been gleaned from a favourite television serial about that era.

Despite Mrs Aylward's initial shock and repugnance at the idea of 'going into service', she had changed her views after meeting her employer and thrown herself enthusiastically into the part of family retainer. Mr Balfour was a sturdily independent seventy-four, and Mrs Aylward adored him and fussed over him with the same devotion that she had given Cathy's father.

'It's me, Mum.' The voice on the other end of the line changed immediately to a soft West Country burr.

'Cathy, love, there's nothing wrong, is there? I was just off to bed.'

'No, don't worry. We townies keep late hours, remember. But I won't be at the flat for the next few weeks, so I thought I'd better ring. We're short of staff at the moment and there's nothing much to do around the office, so I'm going up to Yorkshire on a job. It's all rather a rush—I'm travelling up tomorrow.'

'That'll be nice for you, love.' Cathy doubted it, but said nothing. 'It's not good for you being cooped up in that office all the time. What's the family like?'

'I don't really know yet. From what I've heard, my employer's not the easiest of people to deal with. But it can't be easy for him—it's just him and his daughter. I'm hoping that once I've got everything under control, I might be able to house-train him a bit.'

'Cathy! The expressions you use. So you haven't met him yet, this Mr . . .' There was a note of enquiry in her voice that Cathy recognised only too well.

'Dale, Adam Dale. No, only by reputation. But don't start getting ideas. He's already got a thirteen-year-old daughter, so he's much too old for me. And anyway, I've told you, I'm much too busy with the agency to have time for men at the moment. You'll have to put the matchmaking on hold for a few years.'

Her mother sniffed indignantly. 'That never crossed my mind. But you mustn't work too hard, darling. You're young—you ought to be out enjoying yourself, not working all the time. You don't want to leave it too late, you know. By the time I was your age, I was already married to your father and you were on the way.'

And look how that turned out, thought Cathy silently. He dies before he's fifty and leaves you with no money, no home and no training for any kind of job. And you wonder why I'm not eagerly tripping down the same path.

'You make it sound as if I've got one foot in the grave,' she said out loud. 'There's a year or two of active life left in me yet. And besides, I don't think Dale is going to be son-in-law material.'

'I never suggested he was. I was speaking generally. But you ought to get out more—you never seem to meet any young men. It isn't natural.'

Cathy laughed affectionately. 'Well, I met one today. Nicholas Ballantyne, the one who writes all those books.' Her mother made an indeterminate noise of appreciation which Cathy recognised as meaning that she'd never heard of him. 'He's very famous, anyway, Mum. And very rich. And very, very attractive. He came in to talk me into going up to Yorkshire on this job; apparently Dale is a friend of his. I didn't have a chance. After half an hour, you could have used me to stop the gaps in the window-frames, and Sally was eating out of his hand from the moment she walked in. If you want to exercise your matchmaking powers, I suggest you wave them in his direction.'

Her mother laughed, but her speculative tone wasn't entirely in fun. 'Perhaps he'll come and see you again when you get back. He might want to thank you.'

'Oh, I doubt it. He was just turning on the charm to get what he wanted. I don't suppose I'll ever see him again.'

And perhaps that was just as well. Just talking about him seemed to recall his presence so clearly that she could almost feel his touch . . . his closeness . . . his breath on her hair. Cathy shivered as she said goodnight to her mother. Would she see him again? It was unlikely that she would stay in his thoughts the way he had stayed so vividly in hers. And yet . . . his detailed knowledge of Dale's household and staff problems suggested that he must be a frequent visitor.

It seemed an oddly incongruous friendship, but that was so often the case. No doubt he found something in Dale's lonely farmhouse existence that he needed as an antidote to the sophistication of his London life. Was it too much to hope that he might decide to visit during her stay there? Cathy had a feeling that she might be in urgent need of some civilised company after a few weeks of Adam Dale and his distinctly uncivilised daughter.

She replaced the phone and turned her mind back to practicalities. There was the packing to be done, and then she had to clear out the kitchen ready for her long absence. Resolutely she banished her disturbing visitor from her thoughts and returned to the bedroom.

Re-opening the half-filled suitcase, Cathy realised with a start that so far she had packed her three most precious dresses and no jeans or flat shoes. What on earth had possessed her today? She wasn't usually so absent-minded. Two of the dresses she returned to the wardrobe, but the third, on impulse, she left in. It was a flamboyant creation of brightly printed Indian silks, light and cool and as different from her restrained daytime image as possible without being completely outrageous. Her employer might entertain, unlikely as it seemed. She knew so little about him, after all. Or if Nick came visiting . . .

Cathy clamped down on the half-formed thought as firmly as she closed the lid of the case. She was getting as bad as her mother. Perhaps she should take the dress out? But the straps were buckled; it

THE SEAL WIFE 29

was easier to leave it in. Carrying the case out to the hallway, she prepared to tackle the kitchen.

'Nicholas Ballantyne's latest novel, *China Run,* is his best yet—a fast-moving adventure set in the twilight world of antiques smuggling out of Communist China... it will grip you from the first page to the last. Once again his Oriental backgrounds, like the antiquities his story deals with, have the unmistakable ring of authenticity....'

Cathy turned the thick paperback over in her hand. The front cover depicted a man—the hero, presumably—crouched, aiming a gun, superimposed on a picture of a half-naked Chinese girl with an ornately carved dagger sticking out of her back. The title was written, Chinese-style, vertically down the right-hand side of the page and was almost overshadowed by the author's name at the top. Cathy had picked it up on impulse from the 'number three best-seller' slot on the station bookstall, and now she was wondering why she had wasted her money.

It was emphatically not her kind of book. The cover seemed to promise precisely the mixture of violence and sex that she most disliked. The hero would be the usual tough, hard-hitting international detective; James Bond without the absurd technical devices. But she had liked the idea of reading one of Nick's books, thinking that it would be almost like sharing the train journey with him. And now she had burnt her boats. The train would

be moving off any second and she had nothing else
to read. It was *China Run* or nothing.

By the time she had to change trains at York, a
few of her illusions had been shattered and she
almost wished that she had never picked up the
novel. She found it impossible not to identify the
hero of the book with his creator, and in view of
the subject matter that wasn't a comfortable as-
sociation. She knew that he couldn't really be like
that in real life, and yet . . .

Far from detecting smugglers, the hero was one
of them; a modern pirate living ruthlessly by his
wits, with no allegiance to the law of any country—
or any moral law either, as far as Cathy could make
out. That was something he had in common with
James Bond: the number of beautiful women who
slipped seductively in and out of the story—and the
hero's bed.

And yet, somehow she couldn't dismiss it as just
typical male fantasy material. Something about it
kept her turning the pages, genuinely involved in
the story. Behind the hero's macho behaviour the
plot was gripping, although it took her a while to
feel comfortable about being on the side of the 'bad
guys' for once. And the cover blurb had been right
about the background; it really did ring true. So
that was where Nick had acquired the honey-gold
tan: exploring the Far East in the tax-deductible
name of research. No doubt he had relied on less
personal investigation for the details about the
smuggling rackets. Few writers would think it worth

risking a few years in a Chinese jail for the sake of
authenticity.

As she read, Cathy found her mind drawn inexorably towards other aspects of that 'research'.
How many of those sensuous bedroom encounters
had been drawn from life? She could see again the
writer's hooded green eyes, those full lips, and feel
the animal vitality of his body close to hers, warm
and damp in the stuffy London heat. She was the
woman on the bed in his sleazy Hong Kong hotel
room... He stooped over her and started to un-
buckle his broad leather belt...

She turned the page breathlessly, only to find her
fictional alter-ego with her arms strapped behind
her back, being used as a shield for the hero as he
escaped a shoot-out with a rival gang.

Cathy smiled ruefully and put the book away. It
occurred to her to wonder what sort of books Adam
Dale wrote. Sagas of the depressed North, perhaps?
For the first time, she felt a pang of pity for her
employer. How long was it since he had lost his
wife? It couldn't be easy for him, bringing up a
daughter alone. Which didn't excuse his behaviour,
but did make it more understandable. Perhaps they
would get on all right.

Sweeping her eyes anxiously round the vehicles
parked outside the station, Cathy realised that she
should at least have asked for a description of the
car that was to collect her. Dale had never seen her,
after all, and she had no idea what he looked like—
although she had a very clear mental picture. A

middle-aged Heathcliff, running to seed, was how she imagined him; but that was unlikely to be much help in picking him out in a crowded station.

No, the car was her best bet. Something like a Land Rover, probably—none too clean if farms in Yorkshire were anything like they were in Devon. But unfortunately half the cars in view seemed to fit that description. She spotted one that had a man of about the right age apparently asleep in the driver's seat, so she walked over and peered in at him. The fumes nearly knocked her backwards.

Of course, it would be market day. That was why the place was so crowded. Well, if that was Dale, she would rather he didn't find her; but she didn't think it was. Neither Helga nor Mrs Ironbrand had mentioned that he drank—and she was sure that the latter lady, at least, would not have let such a vice pass without comment.

Just as Cathy was considering asking for an announcement over the station public address system, she heard her name being called. A tall figure climbed out of a gleaming Range Rover which had just pulled up, and came running towards her.

'Cathy, I'm sorry I'm late. Market-day traffic is unbelievable here. I was worried that I'd missed you—Adam would have been furious.'

Cathy could only stare at the new arrival in amazement. It was Nick Ballantyne.

'What on earth are you doing here?' She realised that her tone was almost accusing, as if he was under an obligation to keep her informed of his whereabouts. 'I'm sorry, I didn't mean it to sound like that. But I wasn't expecting to see you up here. I had the impression that you were based in London. Are you staying with Mr Dale?'

'Yes—well, maybe. A couple of days, perhaps; I'm not sure. You're right, I wasn't planning to be here, but something cropped up so I came up this morning. And then I thought I might as well collect you and save Adam a trip. It's almost impossible for him to leave the farm when his daughter is off school.'

He seemed ill at ease, and the explanation rolled out just a little too glibly. Somehow, Cathy received the strong impression that he wasn't telling the truth—but what reason could he have for lying to her? It had to be her imagination.

Nick picked up her small case and swung it into the back of the car. It looked ridiculously tiny on its own in the huge boot space, and Nick looked round for the rest of her luggage.

'I'm impressed,' he said when she indicated that that was all. 'Most of the women I know need a fork-lift truck to pack for anything over a week. Or are you envisaging a speedy return?'

'Oh, no; I'll stick it out as long as Mr Dale remembers his manners.' She sniffed the air appreciatively. 'In fact I'm really quite looking forward to it, having seen the countryside from the train. Is it far from here?'

Ballantyne held the door open as she stepped, or rather, climbed, into the Range Rover. She had never realised before just how high off the ground they were; it was almost like being in a bus or coach.

'About thirty miles. It shouldn't take long once we're out of this traffic.' He clipped on his seatbelt and leaned over to help Cathy with the unfamiliar fastening. As his hand touched hers, she felt a tingle of electricity that made her shiver. He really was devastatingly, dangerously attractive. She was looking forward to her job now, but was it just the unexpected beauty of the scenery? Or was it the knowledge that, for a few days at least, she would be sharing a house with Nick?

Probably she would be so busy that they would hardly see each other, but she would have to be careful. He had already demonstrated his ability to wrap her round his little finger. And, after reading his book, she doubted if he would have any scruples about amusing himself at her expense should country life begin to pall.

By vigorous use of the horn, they forced their way out through the crowded streets and on to the open road. The air was noticeably cooler than it had been in London, with a refreshing moisture that seemed to bring out the smell of the earth. Gradually, the rolling hills on each side of the road grew steeper, with jagged grey cliffs jutting out of the grass. Cathy knew that, close to, the turf would be coarse and tussocky, but from a distance the rocks seemed to be swathed in green velvet, sewn with the thin grey thread of the dry-stone walls.

'It's beautiful.'

Ballantyne smiled at her tone of surprise. 'I think it's the most beautiful place on earth—but it can be one of the most treacherous, too. It's limestone

country; riddled with pot-holes. There are a couple
of impressive specimens at the head of the valley
beyond High Tops—that's the name of the farm—
but don't go exploring without Adam or his
daughter to guide you. I don't want to have to bully
someone else into going to keep house for him.'

They passed through a village of the same grey
stone, which seemed to have sprung from the landscape as naturally as the fells which overshadowed
it. The road became narrower and rougher. Then,
quite suddenly, a dark cloud moved swiftly in from
behind the hill, shadowing the valley and bringing
big heavy spots of rain splashing on the windscreen.

As if to mirror the weather, a shadow passed over
Cathy's carefree mood. The crags seemed men-
acing and she felt very much alone. What did she
know about this man, anyway? Why hadn't he told
her that he would be in Yorkshire? Then another
thought struck her. If he was intending to stay with
Adam for a few days, why did he have no luggage?
She remembered her little case, alone in the boot.
He didn't seem to have even an overnight bag.

A terrible suspicion began to grow. It couldn't
be... But then, these things did happen. You read
about girls being offered tempting jobs by apparently respectable men, and never being seen alive
again. That was why she always made a point of
checking her clients' references so carefully. She had
checked out Adam Dale, but not Nick Ballantyne.
How did she know that he was who he said he was?
He could be anyone. She hadn't even thought to

contact Dale and confirm that he had sent him. She had just accepted Ballantyne's word.

It was ridiculous, of course. But Cathy found it impossible to snap out of her morbid mood and was soon fighting against a rising tide of panic. There must be some way she could check and put her mind at rest, but how? She could hardly ask to see his passport.

A small roadside garage appeared as they turned a corner and the Range Rover slowed down. Thank goodness; he was going to stop for petrol. She could say she had to phone her mother and ring Dale to check. But her relief was short-lived.

'Take a good look at it,' Ballantyne said, driving past. 'That's the last bit of civilisation you'll see.'

'Stop!' she squealed. Her urgency made her driver slam his foot on the brake in an emergency stop.

'What on earth is the matter?'

'I've got to go to the Ladies,' she improvised, scrambling quickly out of the car. 'I won't be a minute.'

To her relief, the garage had a phone in a room not overlooked from the forecourt. Breathing deeply to calm herself, she dialled Dale's number. She was being melodramatic and silly, but never mind. It was sensible to check. But the phone rang and rang and nobody answered. She could hear Ballantyne's voice clearly in her memory: 'It's almost impossible for him to leave the farm...'

There were plenty of possible explanations, of course. He could be outside, too far away to hear the phone. He could be in the bath. But Cathy knew one thing; she wasn't climbing back into that car without checking Ballantyne's credentials, no matter how embarrassing it was.

Screwing up her courage, she marched back to the car and tapped on his window. It whirred smoothly down. 'This is going to sound very silly,' she began nervously, trying to ignore the rain which was soaking into her thin summer blouse, 'but have you any proof that you are who you say you are?'

He didn't react the way Cathy had expected. There was no surprise or indignation—it was almost as if he had been expecting the question.

'And what makes you think that I might be lying?' His tone was one of friendly interest.

'I don't think that at all,' she replied, lying herself now. She was becoming more and more certain that he had something to hide. 'But it just struck me that you've given me no proof that you've actually come from Mr Dale. You could be anyone—I'm sure you're not, but I'd like to make certain.'

Unexpectedly, he started to laugh. 'I'm sorry, Cathy. I'm not laughing at you. I just remembered what I said.' He put on a sepulchral voice. '"That's the last bit of civilisation you'll see..." Did you think I was planning to murder you before the next garage? But no, I shouldn't tease you.' He felt in his pockets and brought out a cheque-book, handing it over with a flourish. '"Nicholas Ballantyne Writing Account", there you go. If I'm a rapist, at least I'm a well-prepared one. The car is Adam's, and I promise that I didn't steal it. Look in the glove compartment: I think he usually leaves his licence there.'

Feeling increasingly foolish, Cathy went round to the passenger door and looked where he directed. Sure enough, there it was. Adam Dale. Her face burned with embarrassment as she clambered back into the car.

'You must think I'm mad.' One thing was certain now. She wouldn't have to worry about the possibility of becoming involved with Nick. If he had had the slightest interest in her before, it was unlikely to have survived being labelled a potential rapist and murderer.

But, to her surprise, he shook his head. 'No— in fact I'm beginning to think you are the first sensible woman I've met. It was brave of you to challenge me. Most people in this country would rather risk death than embarrassment. And you didn't dither; you saw what might be your last chance and took action. What did you do in the garage? You were gone a long time and you don't strike me as being the sort of girl that spends twenty minutes redesigning her face whenever she sees a mirror.'

'I tried to phone Mr Dale,' she admitted. 'I was hoping that he would confirm who you were and then I wouldn't have to tackle you. But he wasn't in.'

Nick nodded approvingly. 'Better and better,' he said. 'I tend to judge people by how well they would perform as a character in one of my books. You'd do all right, especially now that you've left off those terrible glasses. It's a big improvement. If you wore your hair loose, I might even begin to believe your computer's assessment.'

Cathy flushed with a mixture of pleasure and shyness. 'I'm not sure I would like to be a character in one of your books,' she said lightly. 'The women rarely seem to survive longer than a chapter. I was reading one on the train coming up; it's a risky business getting involved with your hero.'

'Life is a risky business. And love especially so.' His tone sounded almost serious and Cathy looked across at him in curiosity, but his next words were as flippant as hers had been. 'Besides, I can't afford to saddle my hero with a permanent relationship. He needs to travel light. Did you enjoy the book? I wouldn't have thought you were a regular reader of mine.'

'I'm not,' she confessed. 'I only bought it because I thought it would be interesting to read something by someone I'd met. In fact, I thought I was going to hate it, but I didn't. Though I do think you could give your women a few more brains. Most of them seem to have an IQ of considerably less than their bust measurement.'

Nick laughed. 'I don't think Mr Average Reader is very interested in their IQ,' he said. 'It's the bust measurement that sells the books—and the film rights. And besides, I told you, I've never met a sensible woman before. I can only write about what I know. Perhaps now I've met one, my next book will sprout a female sidekick. But I promise she won't wear her hair in a bun.'

The rain was heavy now, beating on the roof and windscreen, sealing them into their own little world. Cathy tried to think of an appropriate retort, but nothing came to mind and they lapsed into silence. She resisted the temptation to fiddle with her hair; if it came loose now, he would be bound to misinterpret her action.

She looked across at him, his body relaxed at the wheel, his dark gold mane of hair tumbling round his face, in profile now, his deep-set eyes concentrating on the road ahead. His chin was rough; obviously he hadn't shaved since the day before. It made his elegantly tailored suit look slightly incongruous, like seeing a lion wearing a collar. A lion... her first image of him seemed even more appropriate now. He had set her silly fears at rest, but there was nevertheless an aura of danger about him. 'Life is a risky business,' he had said. She could believe that with him that might be true.

She began to wonder again about his sudden appearance in Yorkshire, and a new thought shaped itself unbidden in her mind. Could it be possible that he had made the journey on impulse, because he wanted to see her again? It was unlikely to the point of fantasy, but the idea persisted. It would explain his awkwardness when he'd met her at the station, and why he had packed no luggage for the trip. And perhaps it accounted for the odd feeling that Cathy had experienced when they'd stopped at the garage, that he had something to hide...

At that moment, as if sensing her thoughts, Nick turned his face towards her and their eyes met. As if a circuit had been completed which connected to somewhere deep inside her, Cathy felt a surge of primitive desire, and knew instinctively that he felt it too. The atmosphere in the car almost crackled. Then he turned back to the road and the contact was broken. Neither of them spoke. Cathy's throat felt dry, but she didn't dare break the silence by swallowing.

Inside her head, thoughts were clamouring for attention. That moment of recognition had passed, but she knew that it had happened. Perhaps she wasn't just letting her imagination run away with her in thinking that he had followed her to Yorkshire. But if it was true, if Nick was interested in her as a woman, what was she going to do about it? Her resolution to let nothing distract her from her work now seemed...naïve. It had been made in cold blood, and there was nothing cold about the blood which pulsed through her veins now, bringing a flush to her cheeks.

His voice broke in, sounding harsher than before. Was he regretting that second of self-revelation?

'Nearly there now.' Even if he hadn't spoken, Cathy would have guessed it from the way the road had narrowed into little more than a track. It was rutted and stony, and the wide body of the car avoided the stone walls on either side by no more than inches. The gradient too had increased.

At last they drew to a halt outside a small clump of stone buildings, nestling in the elbow of the hills behind. As if to welcome them, the rain cleared up as suddenly as it had started and a shaft of sunlight

shone like a spotlight on a pony grazing in the field
behind the farmhouse. Cathy jumped down to undo
the complicated twist of binder twine that, as in
almost every farm-gate she had ever opened, took
the place of a padlock. The familiar action brought
a hot rush of unshed tears to her eyes as she half
carried, half dragged the heavy gate open for Nick
to drive into the farmyard and then closed it again
behind him. For a moment it was as if she was
coming home.

The hens' cackling rose to a warning crescendo
as he slammed the car door shut, but otherwise the
place seemed deserted. Then one of the windows
in the front of the long grey house was thrust open,
and a small figure dropped out. Cathy had no time
to register anything except a mass of tangled blonde
hair as the figure ran towards them and hurled itself
into Ballantyne's arms.

'Daddy!'

CHAPTER THREE

'BECCA! What are you doing here? Why aren't you with Mrs Hallgarth?'

The tangled mop of hair tossed and a pair of crystal-blue eyes flashed dangerously. 'She's horrible; she wouldn't let me go to market with her and she said I couldn't ride Minty unless one of the men went with me. So I waited till she went out and wrote a note to say you were back early. Why do I have to stay with her, anyway? I hate her.'

'Well, you won't now, not for a while at least. I've brought back a new housekeeper to help look after us. Cathy, this is Rebecca. Becca, this is Cathy.'

The child's attention, previously completely focused on her father, flicked over to this new object. Cathy felt the disconcertingly blue eyes bore through her with an unchildlike self-possession. And for a moment she felt a haunting sense of familiarity, as if she had seen those eyes, that face, somewhere before... A painting, perhaps; one of the Pre-Raphaelites? Ophelia floating among the reeds? But it wouldn't come. And the determined hostility of these eyes was decidedly not part of the half-formed memory. Rebecca Dale was plainly her father's daughter.

Her head still spinning with the implications of the situation, Cathy responded automatically. 'Hello, Rebecca.' The elfin face remained stony.

'Say hello, Becca,' her father prompted.

'No, I won't. Why do we have to have house-keepers? I hate them. I can look after you. Anyway, she won't stay. They all go away.' There was a note of gloating satisfaction in her voice as she glared defiantly at the interloper.

Cathy suddenly felt sick and tired of both of them. 'Well, don't talk to me then, if you don't want to,' she snapped. 'But your father had better have his explanations ready.' She turned to the tall figure beside her. 'You've made a fool of me, Mr Ballantyne or Dale or whatever you call yourself, and I would like to know why.'

To her irritation, he didn't seem the least put out. 'Temper, temper. You're as bad as Becca here.' The girl put her arms round his waist and he hugged her tight. 'I had meant to break the news a little more subtly, but as my darling daughter has let the cat out of the bag, I suppose I shall have to confess.' He looked at his wristwatch. 'Nearly six o'clock. Becca, you'd better bring Bonnie in and milk her. I'll show Cathy the kitchen and then come and help you with the feeds.'

Cathy watched the child disappear behind one of the outbuildings and then turned to her father. 'You owe me an explanation,' she said bluntly. 'What was it all about, this farce? Who are you, anyway— Nick Ballantyne or Adam Dale?'

'Let's go inside.' He turned his back on her and led the way into the house by the door which his daughter had spurned. They were greeted by a white-muzzled old border collie who greeted her master as ecstatically as his daughter had done. One eye was milky with age and she almost creaked with rheumatism. Cathy rather doubted that she would have enough teeth left to bite, even supposing her victim was prepared to wait for her to catch up with him. The dog, like the child, ignored her; eyes only for Dale.

She followed the man and his dog into a huge, cluttered kitchen, dominated by an old-fashioned Aga stove at the far end. Slipping off her jacket, she hung it over the back of a chair, then sat down at the table in the centre of the room. 'Well?'

But her host seemed determined to keep her waiting. A kettle of water stood on the side of the stove; he slid it on to the hotplate, waited for the whistle and made a pot of tea. Only when he had poured two mugfuls and set them on the table did he respond.

'Well, what?'

Cathy held her temper in check. He was being deliberately obtuse, but she wouldn't rise to the bait. 'Why did you trick me into coming here? Why did you lie about who you were? Why this whole elaborate charade?'

'This charade, as you call it, was about acquiring a housekeeper. In which it has succeeded. And I didn't lie; my birth certificate may say Adam Dale, but I'm Nick Ballantyne as well, as far as anyone is. It's the name I write under and I generally use it when I'm in London. I prefer to keep Adam's life private. No deceit intended.' He stretched his legs out under the table and smiled when Cathy drew hers primly back. She was tempted to kick him.

'Oh, no,' she scoffed. 'You don't get round me that easily. You didn't just use a different name; you spun me a whole sob-story. If I'd known that you were Dale, I would never have let you talk me into coming here. And you know it.'

'Of course I know it. That was the whole point. I needed a housekeeper urgently—you can see what it's like here if I have to leave Rebecca. And I desperately need more free time to concentrate on my book. But I knew that if Adam Dale turned up at your office, he'd get the same brush-off you gave him by letter, so I thought I'd let Nick Ballantyne sort it out.' He looked at her with something close to contempt. 'It's amazing how it helps to be famous in these situations.'

'That was nothing to do with it! Has it occurred to you that if Adam Dale treated people the same way Nick Ballantyne does, he might get the same results? I admit that I was prejudiced against you and I probably wouldn't have put myself out to help you, but that was entirely due to the way you behaved. Dale demanded, Ballantyne persuaded; that's the difference.'

Adam pushed his chair back from the table. 'This isn't getting us anywhere. None of the things I said as Ballantyne were untrue; I need you just as much as I did when you agreed to come here. And there's not much you can do about it now in any case. I'm certainly not driving you back, and there isn't a bus until Monday. So, unless you fancy a long walk, you might as well start earning your wages and cook us a meal while I go and feed the animals.'

He strode off, leaving Cathy fuming with anger. He had virtually kidnapped her. It had all been a cynical trick. And to think that she had been fooling herself that 'Nick Ballantyne' might actually have found her attractive! Well, there was one comfort—she no longer had to worry about how to react if he did. In the unlikely event of Adam Dale's ever showing the slightest interest, she would know exactly what answer to give. He could go to hell!

She realised that her fists were clenched so tight that her nails were biting into her palms. She took a couple of deep breaths and tried to think what to do next. Unfortunately, Dale was right. She had no transport and they were thirty-odd miles from the station. Even if she had been prepared to risk hitch-hiking, the main road was five or six miles away. For the moment she was trapped.

And, besides, did she really want to go back? She had known all along that she would be working for Dale, not Nick. And she had had few illusions about her employer. Her pride was hurt by the way he had manipulated her, but that was the only difference. As he had pointed out, the arguments still held good: he needed her, the agency needed his money—and she needed a break from London. And, more immediately, she needed something to eat. There was a big chest freezer in the corner of the room. She started to root about in it for something quick to cook.

Five lamb chops were sizzling gently in a blackened old frying pan, and potatoes and vegetables were keeping warm in the slow oven by the time Dale and Rebecca returned. He had changed into an ancient pair of jeans and a baggy Aran sweater. Father and daughter looked tired and dirty.

'It's ready as soon as you've washed your hands.' Cathy announced, with a cheerfulness that wasn't wholly assumed. The atmosphere in the kitchen reminded her of home—of her parents' home on the farm. Somehow, the London flat had never been home. And it was good to be cooking for more than one again.

Adam walked over to the sink, tugging his jersey over his head. He rolled up his shirt-sleeves and sluiced water over his arms and face. Rebecca sat down and started to eat a piece of bread.

'Come on, Rebecca,' said Cathy. 'I'm waiting to dish up.' But the girl's blank expression solidified into mutiny and she sat firm.

'Wash your hands, Becca. I'm hungry.'

At the sound of Adam's soft voice, his daughter jumped up as if the thought had just occurred to her and went over to the sink. The point was unmistakable, Cathy thought wryly. She might have resigned herself to staying at the farm, but their little trio still had one dissident. And one who didn't intend to err on the side of over-subtlety in making her feelings known.

The complete lack of conversation over the meal gave Cathy plenty of time to think out her next move. It was obvious that Rebecca resented her presence. She wanted her father to herself, which was natural enough. At thirteen, she was old enough to feel herself grown-up. No wonder she hated the idea of another woman, a stranger, usurping her position as mistress of the house.

The germ of an idea stirred in Cathy's mind. It was a possibility... and she had to do something. School didn't re-open for another three weeks. Three weeks; sixty-three meals eaten under the unblinking hostility of that piercing gaze. It didn't bear thinking about. She would have to try.

Guessing that Rebecca would slip away as soon as her hunger had been satisfied, Cathy made the first move while the girl was still on her second helping of stewed fruit and custard. She fished in her handbag and brought out a notebook and pencil, then, opening the book at a blank page, said casually, 'Do you want to give me my instructions for tomorrow now? Or would you rather sort it out over breakfast?'

The child stared blankly at her, then looked across at her father. To Cathy's relief, he carried on eating.

'I don't really know what you want me to do yet, you see,' she went on apologetically. 'Or what time you want meals and so on. So perhaps if you just let me know about breakfast, for the time being, and then you can fill me in on the rest of my duties in the morning.'

She sat attentively with her pencil poised over the notepad and said nothing. The silence lengthened and Cathy had to will herself not to break it. At last, Rebecca spoke.

'Seven, we usually have it,' she said in a strained voice. 'After milking. Dad has porridge and I have cereal.'

Cathy wrote it down carefully. 'Right, that's enough to keep me going for now. Could you bang on my door in the morning when you get up? I've been keeping office hours recently, so I might over-sleep.' She started to clear the dishes from the table and carry them over to the sink. 'I don't envy you, trying to keep this place going without help,' she remarked. 'My mother always had at least one woman in from the village. I expect it'll be a relief to get rid of some of the inside jobs so you can spend more time with the animals.'

The only answer she received was another blank look, but that was enough for tonight. Cathy plunged her hands into the soapy water. At least Rebecca had spoken to her without overt hostility. And Cathy had sown the seed of the idea that she was there to help, rather than supplant, the younger girl. It was a start.

To her surprise, Adam picked up a dishcloth and started to dry the dishes as she washed them. She heard the kitchen door slam and realised that they were alone.

'Quite the psychologist, aren't you?' he said sarcastically. Cathy felt her hackles rising, but managed to keep the irritation out of her voice.

'It's part of the job,' she said. 'I'm not being manipulative, not in a cynical way, just tactful. This is Rebecca's house. You're her man—father rather than husband, but otherwise it's no different. She's used to being in charge, so of course she doesn't take kindly to the idea of being demoted to child again. If you're going to take a live-in post, you have to tread carefully.'

Adam looked at her. Cathy wasn't sure how she knew, since her eyes were fixed on the detergent suds in the bowl before her and she didn't dare look up in case their eyes met again, as they had in the car. She didn't want to be reminded that those had been Adam's eyes ...

'So how does a farmer's daughter come to be running an employment agency in London? Was it the call of the bright lights?'

For some reason, his switch from sarcasm to friendliness annoyed Cathy more than ill-temper would have done. She was tired. Why couldn't he leave her alone instead of patronisingly trying to be pleasant? Her answer was bald and abrupt. 'Not exactly. The farm went bankrupt and then my father died of a heart attack. The only useful thing I could do was type, so I came up to London to find a job.' It sounded so simple, put like that. No hint of the humiliating interviews with the bank manager, of the problems of coping simul-taneously with her mother's grief and the loss of her home while trying to find a job that would enable her to support them both. One month she had been a schoolgirl, the next a struggling minnow in a pool that seemed to be filled with piranhas.

'The agency thing just happened by accident. My mother had no training at all; she had never been anything except my father's wife. And she hated London. Then I was sitting on the Tube one evening and overheard two women talking. One of them was saying how sad it was that her father was going to have to leave the home he had lived in all his life because they couldn't find a housekeeper prepared to live somewhere so remote.

'It just suddenly struck me that that was something Mum could do, so on impulse I butted in and said I might know someone. When Mum agreed, the woman offered me a fee—I was staggered. I was just delighted to have found my mother a job; it had never occurred to me that I might charge for it. After that she mentioned me to a friend who wanted a cook, and I realised that there was a market to fill. So I advertised and it went on from there.'

'Very enterprising.'

Cathy looked at him suspiciously. Was he being sarcastic again? 'Well, at least I'm independent. I may not be rich, but at least I know that I'm in charge. I won't wake up one morning to find my whole life in ruins, as Mum did—or if I do, I'll know it was my own fault.'

'Would that make a difference, under the circumstances?'

His tone was strictly neutral, but she thought she could still detect an undertone of mockery. 'I think so,' she said briskly. She didn't have to explain herself to this man. 'That's a pretty searching question for someone who doesn't approve of psychology.'

'I didn't say that. I was just rather surprised that Becca fell for it.'

Cathy heaved a sigh of exasperation. 'Look, I wasn't trying to trick her into anything. I'm genuinely going to need her help if I'm to avoid bothering you with questions. I take it that she knows all the routines?'

'Oh, yes.' There was more than a hint of pride in Adam's voice. 'Do you realise it was yesterday she came back here? I'd asked Hallgarth from the next farm to see to the milking and the stock, but as she told them I was back, he didn't come. She did the lot.'

'You said in the car that I was the first sensible woman you'd met—but maybe you should have said the second.' Cathy spoke jokingly and was disturbed to see Adam's face darken. What had she said to upset him now?

'Sensible, maybe—but hardly a woman yet. She's only thirteen, for God's sake. She'll grow up soon enough. And the chances of an ounce of sense being left inside a head as beautiful as hers are approximately nil.'

'Oh, come on,' Cathy protested, not sure how seriously to take him, 'aren't you being over-pessimistic? She's a pretty child, but she seems level-headed enough to me.'

'We're not talking about prettiness. Rebecca is going to be beautiful—real *"Belle Dame sans Merci"* stuff. Maybe you can't see it yet, but I've seen her future and I know. Power corrupts, and that sort of beauty is power at its most basic. After a few years of seeing half the population swoon at her feet, she'll be as silly, vain and cruel as the rest of them. Let her stay a child while she can.'

The raw pain in his voice was like a bleeding wound. Cathy felt that he was hardly speaking to her, that he had forgotten that she was there. What had happened to cause such bitterness? On impulse, she reached out and touched his arm. The muscle was tense and unyielding under the golden skin, and the hairs which curled under her fingers were crisp to the touch.

'She'll be all right,' she said gently. 'You've done a good job, from what I can see. It can't have been easy alone. How old was Rebecca when she lost her mother?'

Adam's whole body seemed to stiffen. He stared at her uncomprehendingly for a few seconds, then laughed harshly. 'She didn't "lose" her mother, as you so delicately put it. Or only in the sense that an unclaimed parcel in a left-luggage locker can be said to have "lost" its owner. Becca's mother isn't dead—I wish to God she was, it would be better if she were. Mia walked out on us when her baby was six months old. Becca hasn't seen her since. I see her every time I look at my daughter.'

There was a short, strained silence while Cathy tried desperately to frame an apology which wasn't either impertinent or trite. But she was saved the trouble. Her employer threw down the dishcloth and picked up his jersey. His back was towards her. 'Your room is on the right at the top of the stairs,' he said gruffly. 'You'll excuse me if I turn in now; I like to make an early start.' And, before she could even say goodnight, he was gone.

CHAPTER FOUR

CATHY was woken next morning by the sound of a cockerel crowing. In the hazy minutes between sleep and full consciousness, it was as if she was back in her little room at home, with the rosebud wallpaper that had been there when she woke ever since she could remember. Sometimes it happened like that in London, but here the illusion persisted, fed by the familiar sounds of a farmyard waking up. Not until she opened her eyes was it dispelled, to be replaced by a fresh wave of embarrassment at her tactless mistake the night before.

How had she received the impression that his wife was dead? She tried to remember if Helga or Mrs Ironbrand had told her that Adam was a widower, but quite possibly she had just assumed it, since it was so unusual for a man to be left alone to bring up a child by anything other than death. Whatever the excuse, her stupidity had been unforgivable and it certainly wasn't going to make her relationship with him any easier.

She was roused from these depressing thoughts by a rat-tat on the door. Well, that was something at least; she might have alienated the father, but at least his daughter was now prepared to acknowledge her existence. Calling out as cheery a good morning as she could muster, Cathy struggled out of bed and into her clothes. Washing would have to wait. It would be asking for trouble to block the bathroom until she had sorted out Adam's usual routine. They were on bad enough terms without adding that sort of petty irritation.

To her rather guilty relief, the kitchen was empty when she came down and she started to hunt around for the ingredients of breakfast. Milk she eventually tracked down in a separate fridge in the scullery; two huge gallon cans of it, almost too heavy to lift. The cream lay thick and golden on the top and Cathy carefully poured it off into a jug. She wasn't going to lose any weight on this job, which would please her mother. By comparison with her own ample outline, Mrs Aylward saw her daughter's pleasantly curved figure as worryingly thin, and Cathy had long ceased trying to argue with her. She filled a large pitcher with milk and carried it back through to the kitchen.

A movement outside caught her eye and she saw the door of the barn opposite swing open and Adam emerge. He moved slowly, carrying a bucket, and was followed by Rebecca and a sway-backed little cow. The girl had her arm draped affectionately across its neck. So that was Bonnie.

Cathy pushed the porridge to the side of the hot-plate and ran to open the scullery door for Adam.

'You should have left a note, "No milk today, please,"' she joked as he came in. 'How on earth do you get through all this with just two of you?'

'We don't,' he said shortly. 'The pigs and hens take most of it.' Snubbed, Cathy stood back and watched him pour the frothy stream into another milk-can and swing it effortlessly on to the top shelf of the fridge. The last pint or two he held back. 'Put this in the jug for breakfast—chuck the rest in the pig bucket. There's no point drinking yesterday's when we won't get through today's.'

Cathy did as she was told. Although it seemed a terrible waste, what he said made sense. 'Do you make your own butter or cheese at all?' Adam glared at her. Clearly he wasn't in the mood to be friendly after the night before.

'I'm not some self-sufficiency freak,' he said impatiently. 'I'm a writer who just prefers to live somewhere quiet. I bought Bonnie because Hallgarth wanted to get rid of her when her yield went down, and I was sick of driving down to their place every morning to buy milk. I keep a couple of pigs and a few hens because otherwise I'd have to throw half the milk away, and a pony because my daughter likes riding. Now, do you think we could keep the rest of the light conversation until after breakfast? I'd like to make a start.'

This further example of her employer's rudeness extinguished all Cathy's pity for him. No wonder none of her staff had been prepared to put up with it. 'Don't talk to me like that!' she flared. 'I came here as a favour to you, don't forget. I've said I'll stay—but only on condition that you behave yourself. If you think my duties include standing meekly by while you take your bad temper out on me, you've got another think coming.'

'Oh, yes? And what is that?' He had gone dangerously quiet, but Cathy carried on recklessly.

'You think you can get away with intimidating me just because I'm a woman, but you can't. I'm not afraid of you. I won't let you get away with it. You won't drive me away as you did——'

The anger which flamed in his eyes made Cathy step uncertainly backwards, suddenly aware that she had gone too far. 'So you're not afraid of me, are you?' he said, with a quiet savagery that was more terrifying than open fury. 'Well, perhaps you should be. I might decide to see what Miss Self-Assured looks like with her hair down.'

He stroke across the kitchen and seized her as if to shake her, his fingers biting into her arms. Cathy flung her hands up to push him away, but he grabbed her wrists and forced them together, holding them tightly with one rough hand while with the other he tugged at her coiled hair. Its springy fullness fell round her shoulders, spiky with pins.

'That's better. Somehow you don't look so damned efficient now. Not quite a ten, I'm afraid—but definitely attractive.' Before Cathy could turn her face away he pulled her head back and his lips came down on hers; devouring, invading. She struggled and kicked out, but her slippered feet made little impression and he only pulled her closer, twisting his hand in her hair to quell her protests, lifting her nearly off the ground.

His mouth caressed hers; his tongue tracing a line of liquid fire along her lips. To her horror, Cathy felt a response rise in her. She was falling, drowning. The warmth of his mouth was a sea of sensual pleasure, tempting her. She held herself rigid, willing herself not to give in and return his kiss, but her more subtle reactions she was powerless to control. When he finally lifted his face from hers she was flushed and breathless, and her lips felt heavy and swollen with excitement. It must be obvious that he had aroused her.

'Is that the kind of thing you don't intend to let me get away with?' he taunted. 'Still sure you're not afraid of me? That might teach you to keep your poisonous tongue out of my private affairs. God knows what possessed me to mention them to you at all.'

Cathy gasped. No wonder he had over-reacted; he thought she had been about to accuse him of driving away his wife with his temper. 'No! You misunderstood me, Adam.' Her outrage at his behaviour was swamped by her pity. The accusation might even be true, but, in that case, how much more difficult it must be to live with. 'I was talking about the housekeepers I sent you, not—not anything else. I lost my temper, I'm sorry. But I would never be so cruel.'

His muscles gradually slackened as he read the truth on her earnest, upturned face and his grip on her wrists relaxed. 'I'm sorry,' he said. 'I thought— well, I suppose I'm over-sensitive in some areas, and you seem to have a talent for stumbling on them. But I can't say I'm sorry for the result.' He raised one hand and gently stroked the hair away from her face. His touch electrified her skin and she could feel her cheek flood with colour. 'You improve with kissing; nine and a half at least.'

His voice was soft and almost hypnotically compelling. Cathy couldn't tear her eyes away from his face as he bent to kiss her again. Her hands were against his chest where he had held them, but now they were free to move and she could feel the warmth of his body through the rough wool. His touch was gentle now, holding her lightly. She could have pushed him away with ease, but all will to resist had dissolved in the tide of desire which flooded over her. The whole world was his face, his mouth, moving closer and closer to her own. When their lips met, she closed her eyes and prepared to slip back into that warm sea, but the kiss brushed by as lightly as a moth in flight. She looked up in bewilderment at the sudden change.

'We've got company,' he whispered, and then she understood. They sprang apart like guilty teenagers as the scullery door sprang open and Rebecca came into the room. She stopped in her tracks and stared at them, sensing the atmosphere of tension.

'I made Cathy undo her hair,' her father stepped in quickly. 'And now she's cross with me. But I think it looks much better like this, don't you?'

The girl looked at him in surprise, then obediently at Cathy. 'I suppose so,' she said indifferently. 'The other way is better for outdoors, though, or it would blow in your eyes.'

'It's better for housework, too—your father's just being silly.' Cathy started to fumble with the pins, but her hands were shaking and she was even clumsier than usual. 'This is no good; I can't do it without the mirror. Can you serve yourselves? Tea and porridge on the stove and milk and cream on the table. I won't be long.' Before they could answer, she hurried out of the room. She had an urgent need to be alone.

Upstairs, she flopped down on to the hard chair by her dressing-table and stared unseeingly at the mirror. The thought of what had happened, what had nearly happened, throbbed like a drum in her brain. How had he managed to throw her so far off balance? She had been in the house for just over twelve hours, she had known Adam for little longer than that, and yet he had stirred feelings in her that she hadn't known existed and which terrified her with their elemental power.

Nothing had prepared her for that warm, sensuous caressing of her lips, nor for her own unguarded response to it. Just remembering was enough to start her trembling all over again. If Rebecca hadn't arrived, she would have surrendered to her overpowering need for his touch and Adam would have known exactly how far his power over her extended. What sort of working relationship could they have had after that? She would have had to leave, creeping back to the agency to explain to Sally what had happened and ask her to manage on half-wages until the next set of invoices were paid.

Or if she had stayed; what then? After that first surrender, what chance would she have had against a man like Dale if he had decided to amuse himself by seducing her? He was right; she should be afraid of him. His most potent weapon was the traitor within the gates: her own inexplicable desire. And her only defence was to keep him at arm's length, in a purely professional relationship.

Cathy's breathing was gradually returning to normal and she started to pick the hairpins from her hair. Had she really used this many? It felt like a bird's nest. Concentrating hard, she began to re-build her tidy pleat.

Once it was finished, a little lop-sided but still neat enough and with extra pins for security, she sat staring at her face in the mirror. Dale was right, of course. The upswept style emphasised the square, determined set to her jaw and made her full mouth look merely large. But it was practical, and just now the last thing she wanted was to increase her attractions. Camouflage netting might be more appropriate.

Well, there wasn't much more that she could do. She wore no make-up, but her long, dark lashes outlined her eyes as well as any mascara, and the high colour that he had raised still touched her cheeks. If only she had thought to bring her glasses—but they were lying in the office drawer.

She would just have to trust that his work kept him as busy as he claimed, and try and keep out of his way. It wouldn't be easy, especially if Adam kept up the pursuit. But she held one card: he couldn't afford to lose her. He had to behave. And in a month's time it would all be over. She could go back to London and forget about him altogether.

Or you can try, the girl in the mirror seemed to mock. Her own flushed, excited face stared back at her. The memory of Adam Dale might be difficult to dislodge.

Rebecca was alone when Cathy returned self-consciously to the kitchen. 'I'm sorry I was so long,' she apologised. 'I'm terrible at doing my own hair. Was the breakfast all right?'

The younger girl didn't respond, looking so like a wild animal about to bolt that Cathy had to fight an impulse to hold out a palm and make coaxing noises. Instead she went for the practical approach.

'What time do you want me to do lunch?' she asked, stacking up the breakfast dishes. 'And will your father be here?'

To her relief, Rebecca answered almost normally. 'Daddy doesn't want to be disturbed all day. He wants you to leave something outside the study at half-past twelve, but you mustn't knock or go in. He hates it if you break in when he's working.'

Cathy almost laughed at the awe in Rebecca's voice. Probably she had learnt that lesson the hard way. It was somehow reassuring to know that Adam lost his temper with his daughter as well; and as if she had read Cathy's mind the younger girl went on, 'He doesn't mean it, really. He always says sorry afterwards. You have to shout back. That silly fat woman——' Cathy guessed that this was a thumbnail sketch of Mrs Ironbrand '—just cried. I don't cry. Daddy says it's stupid to cry.'

But Daddy isn't a thirteen-year-old girl, Cathy thought. However, it was none of her business how Dale brought up his daughter. She would only be here a few weeks, and then she'd be gone out of both their lives.

'So what else shall I do today?' she said aloud. 'You tell me all the jobs you don't like and I'll put them on my list.'

'I don't like tidying much.' Rebecca looked at Cathy as if half expecting her to argue, and seemed emboldened when she accepted without demur. 'Daddy and me will do the animals and the milking. Daddy likes it and so do I. And they wouldn't know you. And you can do the cooking if you like.'

'That's fine.' Cathy smiled at her young mistress. 'You do the outside and I'll do the inside. But I was wondering if you would have time to take me round and introduce me to all the animals and show me where everything is. I haven't seen anything but the kitchen yet. It doesn't have to be now—I don't want to stop you riding or anything.'

Having her wishes consulted seemed to bring on another fit of self-consciousness in Rebecca, and for a moment Cathy thought she might refuse. But politeness—where had she learned that from? Not her father, surely?—won over timidity and soon Cathy was following her out into the cobbled yard.

It didn't take long to realise that her request had been inspired. On the subject of 'her' animals— Adam she seemed to regard as a mere labourer where the livestock was concerned—Rebecca chattered on with no trace of her former shyness. Soon Cathy had been introduced to the two pigs, called, predictably, Pinky and Perky, and the hens, each of which had been christened for an acquaintance, or enemy, of her guide.

'That one is Mrs Ironbrand.' Rebecca pointed at a large, rather flustered hen being pursued across the run by a svelte black one. 'She used to be called something else, but I changed it because she's always fussing over the other hens' chicks.' She paused, then rushed on. 'She kept calling me her poor motherless chicken.'

Cathy guessed that she wasn't referring to the hen. Rebecca was stubbing the toe of her plimsoll repeatedly against one of the hen run supports. 'I'm not motherless!' she burst out eventually. 'I've got a mother; she's not dead. I asked Daddy and he said she wasn't. She just had to go away—like the seal wife.'

'The seal wife?' Cathy was intrigued and, besides, Rebecca seemed to want to talk. 'Who was she?'

'She was as beautiful as the moonlight on the water. She came out of the sea, and she wanted to stay, but she couldn't. Even though she had a baby. She——'

But at the sound of a neigh from behind the house, the girl's distress was cut off as abruptly as a draught when the door is slammed shut. Rebecca darted off across the cobbled yard. 'Come on,' she called from the gate, looking back. 'Let's go and see Minty.'

After lunch, Rebecca decided to take her pony for a ride out over the fell. She waved cheerfully to Cathy as she left, her earlier outburst forgotten. But Cathy couldn't help remembering the passion in her insistence that her mother wasn't dead and the bitterness in her father's voice the night before. 'She isn't dead,' he had said. 'It would be better if she were...' But he was wrong, at least as far as his daughter was concerned. From her point of view, even a mother she had never seen was better than none at all.

Cathy tried to visualise her own childhood without her mother's cheerful presence, but Mrs Aylward stubbornly refused to fade out of the picture. Cathy made a mental note to phone both her and Sally later that afternoon. But first she would explore the farmhouse and draw up a list of jobs to tackle over the next few days.

The house proved something of an enigma. Although Rebecca's voice was touched with the local accent, not surprisingly as she attended the village school, Adam himself gave no hint of Yorkshire origin. Cathy had assumed since she met him that he had simply bought the house as a conveniently quiet place to pursue his writing. But, looking around, the rooms bore traces of long occupancy—and not just by Adam and his daughter. An ancient treadle sewing-machine seemed to half fill the smallest of the spare bedrooms, and the big attic contained a fascinating hotchpotch of old cream-setting pans, a butter-churn and other reminders of an era when a housekeeper's job would have involved more than merely cooking and cleaning.

Only three of the upstairs rooms showed signs of recent attention. Her own had plainly been cleaned within a few days of her arrival. Rebecca's looked as if had been ransacked by particularly clumsy burglars, with books, toys and clothes lying higgledy-piggledy all over the floor. Cathy didn't go in. If Rebecca wanted her to, she would add it to her list, but until then she intended to respect her privacy. The last, the door at the furthest end of the passage from her own, must be Adam's room. She stood on the threshold, looking in.

It was sparsely furnished and somehow unmistakably masculine, despite the faded floral pattern of the wallpaper. A bookshelf stood against one wall and a single hard-backed chair was positioned by the unmade bed; the chair seemed, from the dirty cups which stood on it, to serve the purpose of a bedside-table rather than a place to sit.

Cathy ran her eyes along a row of books. What was he really like, this man who wrote novels about the Far East from a farmhouse in the Yorkshire Dales? Perhaps his writing had enabled him to live in imagination the adventures that he had been denied by his short-lived marriage and the necessity of caring for his daughter.

The titles were jumbled together; scholarly works on Chinese art and history, copies of some of his own novels, adventure stories by the other famous contemporary names in the genre and a few classics. One particular volume caught her eye—battered, untitled, leather-bound. She pulled it down from the shelf and opened it at random, then realised her mistake. Its hand-written contents proclaimed it to be, not a published work, but a private notebook or diary. The ink was faded and the edges of the thick pages were buckled as if from damp. Her curiosity roused, she tried to read a few words, but they seemed to be in some foreign language; not one that she recognised. She peered at the writing more closely, looking for a clue. It was very odd . . . She heard a movement behind her and stiffened.

'Dusting my diaries, Miss Aylward?'

CHAPTER FIVE

CATHY swung round, her face blazing with embarrassment. 'I—I'm sorry,' she stammered. 'I didn't mean to pry. It was the cover that interested me; I only realised it was a diary when I opened it. I haven't read anything.'

'Obviously not, or you would have realised it was in code.' To Cathy's surprise, her employer grinned broadly. 'Not a very good code, I don't suppose, but at the time it made me feel like James Bond. I could write it as fast as ordinary English. And it served its purpose.'

Realising with relief that she wasn't in disgrace, Cathy laughed. 'Don't tell me your mother tried to read your diary?'

A shadow passed across his face. 'No, it was a bit more serious than that.' He held out his hand for the volume and sat down on the bed, leafing through the pages.

'I must have been mad to write half of this down, even in code,' he said. 'Though I'm very glad now that I did.' He looked up and, seeing Cathy's puzzled expression, beckoned her to sit down beside him on the bed. 'It's my misspent youth, you see—five volumes of it. It's a long story, thank God.'

'Why thank God?' Intrigued, Cathy went over and sat where she could look over his arm at the pages.

'Because these little leather books are stuffed full of the best background material a thriller writer ever had. I never cease to be grateful that I was stupid enough to write it all down.'

He handed the book back to her and she turned the thick, yellowed pages with interest. She could see now that what she had at first taken to be a foreign language was really code; unpronounceable combinations of letters and symbols. On some pages the writing was blurred almost to the point of illegibility.

'It looks as if it has been through a lot with you,' she ventured. 'How exactly did you misspend your youth? Travelling?'

'You could say that.' Adam swung his legs up so that he was lounging the length of the bed. Cathy shifted nervously on the edge of the mattress, but she didn't want to risk breaking the communicative mood that seemed to have overtaken him by suggesting that they should go downstairs.

'Although it wasn't exactly a package tour,' he went on. 'My mother died when I was five and my father and I came here to live with my grandparents. I thought I was in heaven—I loved this place. Then my father remarried and my stepmother insisted that we leave and go down to London. I hated it—and her—just living for the holidays when I could come and stay with my grandparents again. I hardly remember our house in London at all.

Then, when I was fifteen, both my grandpa and grandma died in the same year and my father talked at first of coming back to Yorkshire to live—but she wouldn't have it. She made him rent the farm out; she tried to make him sell it, but there were limits to what even she could force him into. There were no more holidays to look forward to.

'So I did the *Boy's Own* thing and ran away— to sea, if you can believe it. I looked old for my age and I was strong. Gradually I made my way out East and bummed around out there, picking up jobs with anyone who would employ me. I had no papers, so the people who took me on were usually on the shady side.' He grinned again, his eyes narrowing in amusement at Cathy's rather shocked expression. 'Oh, yes—I'm afraid that any- thing Nick Ballantyne's hero gets himself involved in, I've had a swing at as well. Although usually in a rather lowlier capacity. But I kept my eyes open and I kept up my diaries. I hate to think what would have happened if any of my bosses had realised what I was writing down, coded or not. I'd have been lucky if it was only the diaries that went over the side.'

Cathy stared at his face, with its lop-sided smile, trying to piece together the different facets of his character. 'I don't understand; how have you done all this and have a daughter of thirteen? You don't look old enough.' She had forgotten her self- consciousness at his closeness, intrigued by his story.

There was sadness in his answer. 'Well, I'm not exactly Methuselah. I'm thirty-six; I just started young. I spent seven years travelling; then I met Becca's mother. She was only seventeen. I was working a passage as a waiter on a cruise liner at the time, and she was a dancer in the ship's cabaret. I'd never seen anyone so...' Cathy could hear the wonder in his voice, and felt a pang of envy for the girl whose memory, even over thirteen years, could still cast such a spell.

He shrugged. 'I didn't have a chance. And by what seemed like a miracle at the time she seemed to feel the same way. That was when I came home—and found that my stepmother had run off with another man. My father never really recovered. He had moved back up here and I moved in with him, with my wife. Eight months later, I was a father.'

'No wonder you see life as dangerous. Out there, it must have been; and you weren't any older than I am now.' Cathy looked at her employer with something close to awe.

He shook his head. 'Not just out there, Cathy. That's the mistake people make. Life is dangerous anywhere; security is an illusion. The dangers are sometimes different, but they still exist.'

She laughed uncomfortably. Why did he make her feel so vulnerable? He was looking at her now, appraising her in an almost predatory fashion, and Cathy decided it was time for a strategic retreat. She tore her eyes away from him and jumped up. 'You must tell me all about it later,' she said lightly. 'But I mustn't keep you from your work. Would you like me to tidy this room, or do you prefer it left alone?'

Adam jumped up off the bed and walked over to the bookcase. 'Oh, don't let me stop you. You can do it now.'

That was the last thing Cathy wanted. 'No, I'll come back later.'

He smiled slowly. 'So that's one thing you've learnt. You are afraid of me now.'

'No, of course not. I just don't want——'

'Then tidy the room. I'll keep out of your way.'

Cathy realised that there was nothing for it but to go ahead. Well, if he laid a finger on her, she'd make sure that he regretted it. And there wasn't much to do; her employer was obviously a tidy man. She collected the empty cups and stacked them beside the door. Now for the bed. As she bent over to smooth out the sheets, she was acutely aware of the spectacle she must be presenting and wished that her jeans were less tight-fitting. She was convinced that she could feel his gaze burning into her back.

'Why don't you——' She broke off in embarrassment as she swung round and realised that he had his back towards her. Her imagination was really working overtime today.

'Why don't I what?' His tone was so innocent that Cathy almost began to suspect him again, but he seemed to be genuinely engrossed in a book on Chinese architecture. She was making a fool of herself.

'I—er—just thought you could take the other side for me,' she said lamely. 'I didn't realise you were reading. Don't bother, I can manage.'

It didn't surprise her that he made no move to press his help. Whatever else he might be—and she felt now that he might turn out to be anything or anyone—Adam Dale was certainly no gentleman. She finished the bed in record time and moved thankfully towards the door.

'Cathy?' She turned back reluctantly. 'Why are you running away?'

'I'm not.' Her denial lacked conviction even to her own ears.

'This morning, if Becca hadn't arrived, I would have kissed you again. I wanted to do it. You wanted me to. Now we're back to playing games. Why?'

Cathy felt her defences start to crumble as he looked at her, and took refuge in the truth. 'How can I? I'm working for you for a month and then I go back to London. What am I supposed to do; enjoy a four-week frolic in your bed and then wave goodbye and forget all about it? Besides,' she added flippantly, 'since I'm the one who has to make your bed, it's hardly sense for me to help you mess it up.'

'Your mind moves faster than mine. I was talking about kissing. And who says you have to leave? I don't stop needing a housekeeper in four weeks' time. You can stay as long as you want.'

His mention of her employed status irritated Cathy. 'I have an agency to run, remember? And

I'm afraid that even double salary doesn't entitle you to a twenty-four-hour "service"—if that's the word I'm looking for. If you want me to stay here, it has to be on a purely professional basis. Take it or leave it.'

Adam bowed slightly. 'If that's the way you want it. I shall have to make do with watching you make the beds. You looked particularly sexy spread-eagled over mine in those jeans—though without them would have been even better.'

Cathy gasped and flushed in confusion. 'What— but you couldn't see—what do you mean?' Then for the first time she noticed the full-length mirror hanging on the wall opposite the bed. 'You—you're impossible. Why don't you go and do some work?'

'And now you sound more like my agent than my housekeeper. It must be wonderful to be so single-minded. Do call me if you need any more help with the beds.'

Cathy restrained her impulsive retort. Let him have the last word; at least she had made her position clear and he had been forced to accept her terms. She watched him leave the room and waited to hear the study door slam before following him downstairs. She would have to try and avoid being alone with him again.

That, as it turned out, wasn't difficult. Over the next few days, she hardly saw her employer, except at meals, and then he was as taciturn as he had been the first night. True to his claim that he needed to work, he spent all day closeted in his study, and in the long evenings would disappear out on to the moors; sometimes with Rebecca, sometimes alone. Cathy looked enviously after them as they set off up the hill behind High Tops, half hoping that he might suggest that she join them. After his dire warnings about the terrain, she didn't dare venture far out of sight of the farm buildings on her own. But he didn't, and she could hardly blame him. She had chosen the rules of their relationship and she had to live with them. It was just difficult not to feel a little snubbed at the ease with which he relinquished her company.

Rebecca was a different matter entirely; although still shy, she seemed to have lost her initial hostility and settled down into the new routine with a minimum of fuss. So it was all the more surprising when Cathy found her crying in her bedroom one morning, lying face-down on the tumbled bed, trying to stifle her sobs in the pillow.

It seemed best to ignore the muffled 'Go away' which greeted her entrance. 'Rebecca, what's wrong?' There was no coherent reply and she looked around for a clue to the disturbance. Lying by the child's outstretched hand was a screwed-up scrap of cardboard. 'Can I see?'

She took the silence as tacit permission and smoothed out what proved to be a party invitation from a schoolmate for the coming Saturday. What could there be in this to reduce such a stoical child to tears? 'What's the matter, love? Do you want to go? I'm sure I can drive you if your daddy is too busy.'

'I don't want to. They're all stupid, anyway. The
girls all wear stupid clothes and the boys won't let
me play with them any more.' Rebecca sat up, a
woebegone little figure and, impulsively, Cathy gave
her a hug. Emotionally she was very young for her
thirteen years, despite the amount of practical experience she had amassed. To her surprise, the girl
didn't pull away but sat passively while Cathy
stroked her hair.

'Well, if you don't want to, you needn't, surely?
Daddy won't mind, will he?' From what she knew
of Adam, it seemed unlikely that he would force
his daughter to attend. Forbidding it would have
seemed more in character. Rebecca shook her head
mutely, and Cathy knew that she hadn't reached
the real source of the trouble yet.

'Come on, Becca. Tell me about it. Are they horrible to you? Do they tease you about something?'
There had been a quality of defiance in that
'stupid'. Perhaps some of the other children were
bullying her. A renewed burst of sobbing suggested
that she was on the right track.

'They all laugh at me,' Rebecca whispered
eventually. 'Just because they all wear stupid dresses
and I don't. I hate dresses.'

So that was it. 'Well, dresses would be stupid for
round the farm,' Cathy said judiciously. 'But really,
for parties they're all right. I wear jeans all the time
here, but I brought a dress with me as well, in case
I was invited out.' Not that there was any chance
of that now, she thought ruefully. 'Wouldn't it be

worth wearing a dress just for the party? Then they wouldn't tease you.'

Rebecca's voice sank so low that Cathy could hardly hear it. 'I haven't got one, except my uniform. I've only got jeans.'

Cathy felt a surge of indignation against Adam. Didn't he realise what his daughter was going through? He could hardly claim that he couldn't afford to buy her clothes. But then her sense of fairness reasserted itself. Whatever his other faults, Adam plainly loved his daughter and wasn't deliberately insensitive to her needs. He was a man, after all; and until recently Rebecca had probably been perfectly content with her restricted wardrobe. He just didn't realise that she was growing up.

'Have you asked your dad for one?' The answer confirmed her thoughts.

No—I don't want to. Daddy thinks dresses are silly. He says they aren't practical. Mrs Ironbrand tried to make him buy me dresses and he got cross.'

'But that would be for everyday, not for best. I'm sure he wouldn't mind for a party. After all, he wears his special suit when he goes to see his publisher, doesn't he? That's just the same for a man.' So that was Mrs Ironbrand's idea of 'taking in hand'—and the poor child had taken the ensuing argument to heart. 'Don't worry; I'll ask him for you, shall I? I could drive you down to town tomorrow to buy it.'

'No! No, Cathy, please don't.' Cathy couldn't understand her vehemence. 'Please don't ask him;

he'll be cross. I don't want to go to the stupid party, anyway. Promise you won't ask Daddy, please?'

Bewildered, she was forced to give her promise before the younger girl would calm down. It must have been some battle; no wonder Mrs Ironbrand had left. 'All right, I promise. But I'm sure that your dad wouldn't really object. If you change your mind, just tell me and I'll ask him, OK? Now, stop crying and come down to the kitchen. I'm going to make a cake for tea and you can help if you like.' A subdued Rebecca followed her downstairs.

The problem nagged at Cathy all evening, and she had half a mind to forget her promise and broach the subject with Adam. It was ridiculous that Rebecca should be making herself miserable over such a triviality. Perhaps she could find some way of bringing the subject up without actually breaking her word...

But, as if she suspected that Cathy might weaken, Rebecca haunted the kitchen, preventing any chance of a private talk with her father. Not until he finally decided to turn in did she agree to go to bed. Cathy, following them ten minutes later, wondered whether she should speak to Adam in his room. She tiptoed along the passageway and listened at his door. But there were no sounds to tell of his wakefulness and no light showed under the door.

Surely he couldn't be asleep so soon—but she didn't dare risk it. The thought of going in and finding her employer in bed, of having to sit on that same bed while she tried to explain—no, she couldn't do it. From the depths of her subconscious there floated the disturbing information that he slept naked. How on earth did she know that? But, of course, she must have noticed when tidying his room that there were no pyjamas lying around.

It was a simple explanation, but it set the final seal on her decision not to disturb him. She would have to make a chance to speak to him tomorrow.

CHAPTER SIX

'No, I still haven't said anything.' Cathy looked nervously over her shoulder, although she knew that Adam and Rebecca would be safely occupied with the animals for another fifteen minutes at least. The mood her employer was in, she would have hardly dared speak to her mother if there was any possibility of being overheard.

'Then I don't think you should, darling. After all, you did promise and she trusts you.'

'But it's so silly for her to go on being so miserable when he could solve the problem in a flash. I'm certain that she really does want to go to the party; it's just the lack of a dress that's stopping her.'

'But think how angry she would be if you betrayed her confidence, Cathy. You say yourself that she's not just a child; surely she's old enough to make that decision for herself? If she wanted to, she could ask her father. You've promised not to and I think she has a right to your keeping your word. Unless you can find some other way around the problem, you'll just have to leave it alone. She hasn't got anything at all, you say? Nothing outgrown that you could alter? Or even a pretty nightdress?'

'She wears pyjamas, and I don't think she can ever have possessed a dress. I even looked through the linen cupboard to see if there was a patterned tablecloth or something that I could use, but it's all plain white. She'd look like a bride—or a corpse.'

'Oh, dear. It's not right, a man having to bring a girl up alone. They just don't think of these things. And when I think of the fun I used to have dressing you up when you were little. I wonder why Adam—is that what you called him, dear?—has never remarried.'

Cathy sighed. She might have known that her use of her employer's first name wouldn't go unnoticed. 'I told you, Mum, don't start getting ideas. I'm keeping him at arm's length and, anyway, he wouldn't be interested in marriage. I should think Nick Ballantyne has quite a string of admiring ladies to keep him happy, even if Adam Dale is a bit of a hermit. And besides, he still hasn't got over his first wife leaving him, if you ask me. There's still so much bitterness when he talks about her; after thirteen years, you'd think it would have faded.'

'Well, she sounds to me like a very unnatural woman and I'm not surprised he's bitter. People don't expect men to be sensitive, but they are.'

'Sensitive! If you'd had to put up with him today, Mum... I don't know what's got into him, but neither I or Rebecca can do a thing right.'

'I expect he's got worries, dear. Business or something.' Her mother's comfortable tone made it sound like some alien disease, contracted only by the male sex. 'Men have so many responsibilities, and worry does make them bad-tempered. I remember your father... And it must be difficult to have no one to share it with. He'll get over it just as soon as he meets the right woman, I'm sure, but it's a shame for his daughter that it's taking him so long. Say what you like, a girl needs a mother.'

'I wouldn't dream of contradicting that,' Cathy said fondly. 'I don't know what I would do without you, even now. And I'm sure you're right about the dress—I won't mention it to Adam. But I must go now, Mum. It's his phone bill and I don't want him to think I'm taking advantage. Bye-bye—I'll call you in a couple of days. Give my best wishes to Mr Balfour and don't work too hard.'

'Goodbye, dear. I hope you work something out. And don't be too rough with poor Mr Dale. He sounds like a sensitive man, and you can be rather—well, forthright at times.'

Mrs Aylward rang off, leaving Cathy half amused, half stunned. How on earth had she given her mother such a misleading impression of her employer? He was about as sensitive as a rhinoceros, to her, at any rate. If he had an Achilles' heel, it was his feeling for his wife—ex-wife. It was unlikely that any dents her own 'forthright' behaviour might make in his armour would last once she disappeared from the scene. She was surprised to realise just how much that hurt.

Seconds later, there was a roar from the cowshed, mixed with the clatter of a metal pail on cobbles. 'That bloody cow!' Sensitive! If only her mother could see him now. It was almost as if he

had overheard their call and set out to prove her
wrong. Cathy felt her irritation mounting. Why
should the whole household suffer just because he
had writer's block or whatever? And as for the
possibility of him having 'business worries'—any
worries the famous Nick Ballantyne might have
were more likely to be with spending money than
making it.

She watched him stalk back across the yard with
an empty bucket and heard it clatter into the
scullery sink so loudly that she winced for the
enamel. Behind him followed Rebecca, her face set
and as mulish as her father's, pointing out that it
wasn't Bonnie's fault that he had left the full pail
where she could kick it over. They made a good
pair.

The meal was eaten in tense silence, punctuated
only by the occasional grunted request from Adam.
Cathy was forcefully reminded of the first evening
of her stay—only this time it was Adam who was
acting like a spoilt child. Rebecca, obviously a
veteran of her father's moods, disappeared off to
her room as soon as it was over. Ironically, she
could now have had the private talk with Adam
that she had wanted the night before. Except that
even if her mother hadn't convinced her that she
should respect Becca's wishes, she would have
known instinctively that now was not the time to
ask her employer for anything.

He made no move to help her with the washing-
up, but nor did he seem to be preparing to go for
his usual evening walk. Cathy wondered if he in-

tended to sit and stare into space all evening. She hoped not. He made her feel jumpy and uncomfortable, gazing morosely through her as if she didn't exist. She hurried through her chores, resolving to leave him to it and retire to read in her room.

'Don't go.' There was a note of pleading in his voice that arrested her. 'I could do with some company.'

In spite of her irritation at his childish behaviour, it was impossible to refuse such a direct request. 'You could have fooled me,' she said bluntly, turning back from the door. 'You've hardly spoken a civil word to either of us since breakfast. What's the matter? Isn't the book going well?'

'What? Oh, no—the book's fine. In fact it's well ahead of schedule. But I could do with a drink, and I don't like drinking alone. It's been a depressing day.'

'A walk would do you more good. Alcohol's a depressant.'

'Yes, Doctor.' He grinned at her with something more like his normal spirit. 'But I was thinking of combining it with a game of cards. How would you like me to teach you the finer points of crib?'

Her first impulse was to refuse, but when she saw his face drop she changed her mind. Perhaps her mother was right—and, besides, she might even win. He couldn't suspect that she had been brought up on the game. Beating Adam Dale at something was an experience not to be missed.

*   *   *

Cathy sat in the little front parlour, sorting through the cards in her hand and remembering all the games she had played with her father. She watched Adam fiddling with the peg-board. 'So what was depressing about today, if the book is going so well?' She deliberately kept her voice light. Something told her that he wouldn't appreciate her pity.

'Nothing that you need worry about.'

The flat rudeness of his rebuff made her gasp, and cut off the trickle of her sympathy like turning a tap. Slapping the cards down on the coffee-table, she heaved herself out of the armchair and stood up. 'In that case, I'll take my drink upstairs,' she said coldly.

'Don't be so childish. Sit down and play your hand.'

'Childish? Me?' For a moment, indignation seemed to dam the words in her throat. 'You've been in a foul temper all evening. You've snapped at me, you've shouted at the animals, and how Rebecca isn't in tears I don't know. Then you drag me in here on the pretext of wanting some company and proceed to bite my head off when I ask a perfectly normal question.'

'I'm sorry. It's just—'

'None of my business; yes, I know. You made that perfectly clear. Well, let me make something clear, Adam. I don't have to put up with your rudeness. I'm doing you a favour, remember?' Cathy mentally crossed her fingers, remembering how low the agency bank account would have been without his generous advance payment. What if he called her bluff? But if she let him get away with it now, he would walk all over her. 'If you can't behave like a reasonable——'

'My solicitor phoned this morning. They want to take Becca away from me.'

The stark words were like a winding blow. Cathy stared at him aghast, unable to take in what he was saying but only aware that once again she had made a terrible mistake. Dazed, she sank back into the chair. 'What . . .?'

'Oh, not kidnapping or anything uncivilised like that. It's for her own good, after all. All they have to do is prove that I'm not a fit father for her.' He picked up the rest of the pack of cards and riffled through them distractedly.

'But that's ridiculous, Adam. You've looked after her all her life. No one could claim——'

'Couldn't they? Her mother——' he almost spat the word '——thinks differently.'

'A woman she hasn't seen since she was a baby? You've got this all out of proportion, Adam. From what you've told me, she hasn't a chance. She walked out on you both, didn't she? And she's never taken any notice of Becca since then. No court in the country is going to give custody to a woman like that, especially after all this time.'

'Not even to Mia Tannabrae?'

Mia . . . Mia Tannabrae. Of course. That haunting likeness that Cathy had seen in Rebecca. An Ophelia, yes—but not a painting. An actress; one of the greatest Shakespearean actresses of all time, they said, and one of the few who had successfully made the transition to film. That elfin face; and those eyes. It was so glaringly obvious, except that she would have said the actress was too young to have a daughter of thirteen. But then Adam looked hardly old enough himself. They had both been very young. Young and in love... on Adam's side, at least.

He broke in on her thoughts. 'It makes a difference, doesn't it? Can you imagine her in the witness box, telling the world how she gave her daughter away because she believed it was the best thing for her; only now to realise her mistake? She does that sort of thing so well, doesn't she? Look at that last film of hers—in fact, I think it was playing that role that put it into her head. The tragic mother, forced by circumstances to abandon her children. She hardly needs to appear in court; she could just send them a video copy of the final scene. You do see that it's bound to make a difference?'

Cathy did see. 'But even so, Adam, unless she can show that Becca is unhappy with you or that you ill-treat her, surely there's nothing she can do?'

'Well, my solicitor is worried. If I had married again, it would have been different, but as it is, he thinks they could make ammunition out of my life here; make me out to be some sort of unhealthy hermit—letting her run wild, in need of care and control; that sort of thing. Unfortunately I've never hit it off with the old bat at Becca's school. She's probably prepared to swear that I eat Mixed Infants for breakfast.'

He smiled wryly. 'They might even dig up some of my previous housekeepers. If it comes to court, there's just a shadow of a chance that she might win—and even if she doesn't, Becca's life won't be private any more. "Actress and Novelist in Love-Tug Drama." You can imagine what the papers will make of that.'

'So what will you do?'

'At the moment, nothing. The lawyers say that I should meet her half-way—give her access, let them get to know each other—but I'm damned if I'll do that. I won't have her poisoning my daughter's mind. And anyway, I know Mia; she never did have a very long attention-span. She works herself up into a part, and at the moment it happens to be bereft motherhood. In a few months' time she'll meet a new man or be offered a new role, and she'll start to realise that a thirteen-year-old daughter is bound to cramp her style. As well as making it embarrassingly difficult to stay an eternally youthful twenty-nine.'

His voice was light and mocking, with only a hint of the despair and helplessness that he must feel. Cathy felt her heart go out to him. She still couldn't really believe that a court would take Rebecca away—but the mere possibility must be torture.

And it must be so much more difficult for you, she thought, watching his tense figure hunched over the low table. You've always been able to take what you wanted, by charm or by force. Except her. And now your weapons are as useless against this new threat as they were when she left you. It can't be easy for a pirate to take a back seat and let his solicitors play a waiting game.

'I'm sorry, Adam.' Her words sounded hopelessly inadequate. 'I didn't know.'

He shrugged. 'How could you? And you were right, I had no business taking it out on you. You and Becca seem to hit it off well; it's been a weight off my mind. My solicitor keeps telling me how important it is that I provide a "stable background".'

'That makes me sound like a horse.'

His lips twitched. 'You do me good, Cathy. I'm glad I told you—it puts things back in proportion. But not a word to Rebecca, please. I hope she'll never have to know.'

'But surely one day——?' Cathy remembered again Becca's wistful face when she spoke of her mother.

'Perhaps. But not until she's older and strong enough to cope. Now would be the worst possible time; she's just beginning to grow up; her personality is still forming. I don't want her exposed to that sort of influence.' A fierceness had begun to creep back into his voice, but he checked it and smiled. 'But that's enough about my problems. On to the important things in life—I believe I was about to give you a cribbage lesson.'

'Oh, yes,' said Cathy innocently, rejoicing inwardly at his change of mood. 'I believe you said you were.'

'You, Miss Aylward, are a hustler.' Adam gathered up the cards as Cathy moved her peg into the

winning hole. ' "Played a few times", indeed. Next
time I shall stop being kind to you. This is a dec-
laration of war.'

'Oh!' Cathy scoffed. 'That's your excuse, is it?
Being kind to me? That's about as likely as a lion
being kind to a gazelle. I beat you fair and square,
so don't try to wriggle out of it.'

'You've got me all wrong.' He looked at her with
mock reproach. 'And your natural history is all to
pot as well. Don't you know that it's the lionesses
which do the killing? Kipling had it right: "The
female of the species is more deadly than the male."
We poor males are much too sensitive for all that
tooth and claw stuff; we just learn to roar as loudly
as possible and hope that no one sees through the
façade.'

'You must have been talking to my mother; she
seems to have got the idea that I'm bullying you.'

'She sounds a sensible woman. I bet she wouldn't
beat me at crib.'

Cathy shook her head. 'Now I know you've been
talking to her! My mother never won a game in her
life except by accident, and then she'd spend the
next two hours explaining how it was all down to
luck. She used to play my father at draughts every
night, and I could never understand how he didn't
realise that she was cheating in his favour all the
time.'

Adam grinned. 'I think I'd get on well with your
mother. Ask her to stay while you're here if you
like—it'll be company for you. I'll pay her fare.
After Rebecca goes back to school, I'll probably

have to go down to London again, to discuss the
final version of my book and I might be away a
few days—it's a lonely place to be on your own.'

His unexpected consideration left Cathy with
mixed emotions. On the whole, she thought she
preferred the lion to roar. At least then there was
no doubt just where the danger lay.

CHAPTER SEVEN

IT WAS dark, and Cathy lay awake with the vague, uneasy feeling at the back of her mind that something had woken her. She held her breath, listening intently. Yes, there it was again. Sobbing. She slipped out of bed and crept along the passage to Rebecca's room, listened for a moment to confirm her suspicions and then let herself into the room.

Rebecca's curtains stood open and the room seemed almost light after the blackness of the passageway and her own curtained room. 'It's me— Cathy,' she whispered. 'Don't cry, darling. Do you want—— Oh!' Her exclamation dissolved in amusement as she investigated the sharp object under her foot and identified it as a scale model of a combine harvester. 'I'm not sure I can reach the bed without a map, actually. If I'm not there in twenty minutes, send out the Fell Rescue, will you?' She tiptoed gingerly through the rest of the minefield and sat on the bed, rubbing her foot.

'Ow! Why does it always hurt so much more when your feet are cold? These floors are freezing at night.' She looked down at the child in curiosity, intrigued by her new knowledge. Mia Tannabrae's daughter... The likeness was certainly there, so strong that she wondered how she had ever missed it.

But then a smile crept over the girl's wan little face. 'You can come in here, if you like,' she said, pulling back the covers and moving over towards the wall. And suddenly Cathy could see only Rebecca, uniquely and enchantingly herself.

Touched by the gesture, she tucked her feet up into the bed and smoothed the covers back over the two of them. 'Now, what's the trouble, Becca? Are you still worrying about that party?'

Rebecca shook her head mulishly and, in an obvious attempt to change the subject, reached out and touched Cathy's loosely hanging hair. 'Daddy liked your hair like this.'

'Yes; well, as I said, it's not very practical for housework. But if I was invited out somewhere special, I would wear it like this to go with my dress.' Cathy felt quite proud of the neat way she had brought the conversation back on target. But Rebecca was not so easily manipulated.

'I like it too,' she said, as if Cathy hadn't interrupted. 'And I like your nightie.' She fingered the lace edging round the neckline. 'It's much prettier than my pyjamas.'

Cathy looked down at the delicate Liberty print; a trophy from the January sales. 'You've just given me an idea,' she said slowly. 'I bet you didn't realise I was a fairy godmother, did you? Cinderella, you shall go to the ball. How would you like it if I made you a dress out of my nightie?'

But Rebecca was not easily persuaded. Although her eyes had sparkled with interest when Cathy first

made the offer, she was still convinced that her
father would disapprove.

'I'll tell you what we'll do,' offered Cathy at last.
'We'll make it a surprise for him. We can both dress
up—I'll put my party dress on as well. Then it won't
be just you. Would that make you feel better? And
I'll tell him that the dress is a present from me to
you—he can't get cross about a present. When's
your birthday?'

'Not until March.'

'Then it will have to be an un-birthday present,'
Cathy said firmly. She could feel Rebecca
weakening.

'Like Humpty Dumpty in *Alice Through the
Looking Glass*. Daddy used to read that to me when
I was little.'

'There you go, then. How can he complain about
an un-birthday present in that case?' Rebecca
giggled. 'Honestly, I'm sure it will be all right. And
even if he did get cross, it would be with me, not
you. And I don't care. I'll just do what you said
and shout back.'

'You won't leave, like the others?'

'Well, not because he shouts at me. I'm staying
for another few weeks yet. But I can't stay a very
long time—I've got another job to do in London.'
Rebecca looked as if she might cry again, and Cathy
gave her another hug. Poor kid, it must be lonely
for her up here if she was so ready to attach herself
to someone she had known less than a week.

'Don't worry, Becca,' she whispered. 'Now that
I know you, I'll make sure I send you someone nice

GET 4 BOOKS

FREE

Return this card, and we'll send you 4 brand-new Harlequin Presents® novels, absolutely FREE! We'll even pay the postage both ways!

We're making you this offer to introduce you to the benefits of the Harlequin Reader Service®: free home delivery of brand-new romance novels, months before they're available in stores, AND at a savings of 26¢ apiece compared to the cover price!

Accepting these 4 free books places you under no obligation to continue. You may cancel at any time, even just after receiving your free shipment. If you do not cancel, every month we'll send 6 more Harlequin Presents novels, and bill you just $2.24* apiece–that's all!

Yes, please send me my 4 free Harlequin Presents novels, as explained above.

Name

Address   Apt.

City   State   Zip

106 CIH BA59 (U-H-P-07/90)

DETACH ALONG DOTTED LINE AND MAIL TODAY! – DETACH ALONG DOTTED LINE AND MAIL TODAY! – DETACH ALONG DOTTED LINE AND MAIL TODAY!

Get 4 Books FREE
SEE BACK OF CARD FOR DETAILS

to be your housekeeper once I've gone. And I'll be here until after you go back to school, I promise. However much your Dad shouts at me.'

'And why should I shout at you? I thought we'd settled that it was you who were bullying me.' Adam had entered as quietly as a cat and now stood by the bed, looking down at them in amusement. 'Don't you worry about Cathy, Becca. She's got me well under her thumb. If I shouted at her, she'd probably hit me with the frying pan. What have I interrupted here, anyway? A midnight feast? Where are the buns?'

'We were just talking,' Cathy said with dignity. 'Rebecca had a bad dream.'

'What, no buns? Stay there.' Adam hurried out of the room.

'What on earth is he doing? He must have gone mad—it's two o'clock in the morning. I'd better go back to bed.' Cathy went to climb out on to the cold floor, but Rebecca pulled her back, her eyes dancing with delight.

'You can't go now; we're going to have a feast! Daddy and I used to have lots of feasts, but it's ages since the last one. I thought perhaps I was too old now.'

'Well, if I'm not, I should think you've a few years to go yet. Are you sure I'm invited?'

'Of course you are!' Rebecca looked at her reproachfully. 'But don't tell him about the secret, will you? I want it to be a surprise.'

Cathy smiled with pleasure. 'Then you will? Oh, good, I'm so glad. I'll make it tomorrow while he's working and we can show him tomorrow night. You'll be the prettiest——'

'Sssh! Daddy's coming!'

Adam re-entered carrying a tray of cake, biscuits and the pork pie that Cathy had earmarked for the next day's lunch, and deposited it on Cathy's lap, effectively pinning her to the bed. Then he disappeared again and came back with an ice-bucket, containing to Cathy's stunned amazement a bottle of champagne and a carton of orange juice. He set it down by the foot of the bed and produced three glasses from the pocket of his dressing-gown.

'Tea, vicar?' He uncorked the champagne and caught the first surge of bubbles in a glass which he passed with exaggerated politeness to Cathy. He opened the carton of orange juice and held it poised over her drink. 'Milk?'

'Yes, please.' At least the addition of orange made it seem more like an early breakfast. She noticed that he poured the same for himself and his daughter, although Rebecca's glass was less than half-full before he added the juice.

'Mind your drinks!' Cathy had scarcely time to grab hold of the tray before the covers at the foot of the bed were pulled back and Adam's bare, muscular legs and cold feet were invading their warm space. Rebecca shrieked in excitement and began to kick at him under the covers.

'Whoa, whoa! You'll make Cathy drop the food and I'll spill my drink. This is a midnight feast, not a chimpanzees' tea-party.'

Cathy sat rigid, afraid that the slightest movement would bring her legs into contact with his. He made Rebecca's bed seem ludicrously small; sitting propped against the rail opposite her, the bump his feet made in the covers was level with her knees. But then most single beds would seem small with three people in them, she reminded herself. How on earth had she found herself in such an incredible position? In bed with her employer drinking Bucks Fizz at two in the morning—how debauched it sounded! And yet the reality was so different.

The incongruity of it all fought against her shyness and won. It was a situation too crazy for normal rules to apply. To Adam and Rebecca, this was obviously the most natural thing in the world: warm, loving and spontaneous. She wasn't going to spoil it for them. 'I think you're both completely mad,' she said, raising her glass. 'But cheers.'

Most of the food and a surprising quantity of the champagne had disappeared by the time Rebecca's eyelids finally gave up the struggle against gravity. Cathy felt as if she was floating beyond tiredness in some realm of peace where sleep was no longer necessary. It occurred to her that she had probably had too much champagne. She climbed carefully out of the bed and stood up, only to sit down again quite suddenly with the room spinning round her head.

'Look at this, Becca,' Adam teased. 'Our house-keeper is drunk. I shall have to complain to the agency.'

'I'm not drunk, I just stood up too quickly.' Cathy was aware of having to take rather more trouble than usual to form her words. 'All the blood ran away from my head.'

Then Adam was beside her, scooping her into his arms. 'We can't have that,' he said gravely. 'Who knows what might take its place? Pure champagne bubbles, most likely. Anything might happen. I'd better put you to bed.'

It seemed all of a piece with the dreamy feeling in her head that she should be in Adam's arms. He carried her along the passageway as if she weighed no more than a child, and with a child's innocence she lay passively against his breast, enjoying the strength of his arms around her and the warm, masculine scent of his body through the cotton robe.

'Do you always drink champagne at your mid-night feasts?'

He set her down gently by her own bed, but his arms were still around her and he looked down at her with something in his eyes that made Cathy suddenly intensely aware of her own womanhood. She wasn't a child. And Adam was very much a man.

'Never before. Tonight was a celebration.'

'Because the book is going well?'

He shook his head. 'Much more than that.' He was still looking at her as if he would consume her with his eyes. For a moment, Cathy's world stood still, then slowly began to revolve again in the opposite direction. His next words sent it spinning crazily out of control.

'I'm falling for you, my lovely Cathy. I want you so much. Seeing you sitting there in bed with Rebecca—I was drunk without the champagne.' His voice was touched with wonder. 'You seemed to belong there. You fit in; you're part of the family. And you're so beautiful.'

The last word was no more than a breath as their lips met and merged into one passionate devouring. Cathy felt as if every champagne bubble was exploding simultaneously in her head. Her legs buckled and he lowered her gently down on to the bed, leaning over her, one hand on each side of her head. She reached up in wonder and touched his chest where the robe was slipping open.

His voice was urgent. 'There's something special between us, Cathy. And you feel it too, don't you?'

'Yes.' Cathy wondered how she had ever not known that she loved him. It was as if it had taken her twenty-three years to notice that her eyes were brown. Mesmerised, she traced with her hand the line of crisp golden hair that trailed down from his chest, down to the knotted belt of his robe, and beyond. He caught at her wrist.

'Don't tempt me.'

'I love you, Adam. I want you.' There was no shame in the admission, just the naked honesty of truth.

He shook his head. 'Not now; not tonight. I can wait.' He grinned at her, and the lop-sided smile made her heart turn over with desire. 'The first time we make love, I want to be sure that you'll remember it in the morning.'

'You beast!' She started to struggle up, but he pushed her back and sealed her mouth with a kiss.

'I want it to be perfect, Cathy. I promise it will be worth waiting for. Trust me.' Gently he pulled the covers over her and tucked them in. Then he kissed her lightly on the forehead and was gone. And Cathy, convinced that she would never sleep, slipped peacefully into oblivion.

She woke the next morning with a headache and the feeling of having surfaced out of a dream that she wished could go on for ever. Still dazed with sleep, she burrowed down under the covers and tried to recapture it. Adam, bending over her. Adam's words caressing her. Adam kissing——

Suddenly she was fully awake and aware of two things. One, that it hadn't been a dream. And two, that she had overslept. The sunlight pouring through her curtains lacked the delicate quality of the early-morning light and the room was hot and stuffy. She made a grab for her watch from the bedside-table, nearly knocking over as she did so the delicate glass vase which stood there, its tall, cut-crystal sides supporting a single red—tomato. Cathy stared at it in disbelief, but it remained obstinately a tomato. It certainly hadn't been there the night before, and she couldn't imagine what it was doing there now.

But when she looked at her watch, what she saw banished the unusual table decoration from her mind. Past midday! Adam would be wanting his lunch any minute...she had promised to make Rebecca a dress...and the day was half over already. Evading the other, more disturbing thoughts which clustered for her attention, she jumped out of bed, groaning as the movement seemed to set off a small hammer somewhere in the centre of her forehead. Practicalities first. The rest could wait.

But the house was suspiciously quiet, and when she reached the kitchen she found out why. A note was placed prominently on the kitchen table, propped in place with a bottle of headache tablets.

> 'Cathy—Rebecca and I have gone shopping—back about three. Hope you don't feel too bad,
>
> Love, Adam

Gone shopping? Did that mean that Rebecca had plucked up the courage to ask her father for a dress, or had he just decided to take her on his normal weekly trip into town so that Cathy could lie in? Probably he had guessed that she would need time to think... Cathy's mind shied away again from the memories which that threatened to recall. There was a warm glow of happiness nestling somewhere inside her ribcage, but she had a feeling that too much thought might just dispel it.

She pushed the kettle on to the hotplate and took two tablets from the bottle, swallowing them with a glass of water. If she didn't examine it too closely, the warm glow might last a little longer. She sat down, cradled her head on her arms, and waited for the hammers to subside.

She managed to hold off the thoughts until she actually started sewing. Her spare nightdress lay dismembered on the table. It was the twin to the one she had worn the night before except for the colour, a forget-me-not blue which would be perfect for Rebecca. The sizing she had taken from one of Rebecca's shirts, so it ought to fit, and any fine adjustments could be made when the girl returned. She glanced at her watch. Only an hour to go.

Soon her feet were working rhythmically as the ancient sewing-machine worked its way along the seams of her creation. It was a mechanical task, keeping her hands occupied but leaving her mind free to roam. Her headache was almost gone, and what remained Cathy suspected was more due to the oppressive heat than the after-effects of the champagne. Surely it was hotter today than it had been before, even in London? Her hands were damp as she handled the delicate cotton, and her skin felt prickly and uncomfortable.

There was no longer any excuse not to think about the implications of the previous night. Every moment, every word, every touch was vividly stamped on her memory. He had said she was beautiful. He had kissed her... The sensations flooded back, so intense that her feet faltered and lost rhythm, making the old-fashioned machine stitch backwards until she brought it under control.

And she had told him that she loved him... Cathy groaned and felt her face burn with shame and embarrassment as that memory too came back to haunt her and she recalled just how uninhibited her confession had been. Freed by euphoria and the effects of the champagne, she had wanted him desperately—had virtually tried to seduce him, in fact. So much for the 'purely professional relationship' she had been so determined to foster. She had only Adam to thank for the fact that she had woken up alone.

Why, oh, why had she given herself away so completely? What on earth had possessed her to say—that word? Only last night, when he had looked at her like that and turned her world upside-down, it had all seemed to make perfect sense. 'I'm falling for you,' he had said—and she had soared to the conclusion that he meant falling in love. His touch, his kisses and his gentleness had seemed to confirm it.

But he hadn't said that. That was the worry that had been nagging at the back of her mind. She could have repeated every word that had passed between them, and the only person to mention love had been herself. In sober daylight, Cathy had to admit that nothing he had said to her was indicative of anything more than she already knew—that there was a special chemistry between them; an attraction that they both found difficult to resist. That

Adam, as he had made plain before, had no desire
to resist. But not love—or, at least, not on his side.

'I love him.' She whispered it through dry lips,
and knew with terrible clarity that it was the truth.
Lulled by champagne and false hopes, she had let
herself step over the barriers which were all that
had kept her safe from her own feelings. She had
fallen headlong into love and now she could no
more hope to go back than if she had fallen off a
cliff.

Her headache started to throb again as she con-
templated what she had done. If it hadn't been for
the champagne she would never have been such a
fool as to believe that Adam—that Nick
Ballantyne—could possibly be interested in more
than an affair. How could she hope to follow Mia
Tannabrae? Especially when none of the far more
glamorous women who no doubt surrounded him
in London had been able to exorcise her ghost.

How naïve she had been. She remembered, with
pain, the amusement on his face when he'd kissed
her goodnight, and supposed that she ought to be
grateful that he had been enough of a gentleman
not to take advantage of her state. But what must
he think of her? And however was she going to face
him on his return?

The turmoil in her mind was too painful to bear
and she wished desperately that she could just go
back to bed and wake again to find it had never
happened. But the hands of the clock were moving
inexorably towards the moment she was dreading.
Well, at least she could ensure that Becca's dress

was ready. Burying the disturbing memories as deeply as possible, she turned back to her work.

She heard the Range Rover before she saw it; the purr of its engine carrying clearly on the still, close air. The dress was finished except for the hem, which would have to wait until Rebecca could model it. Cathy felt quite proud of her inventiveness as she held her work up for inspection. The overall effect was rather like a Laura Ashley design, Victorian in flavour. All in all, it had turned out rather well.

Then the sound of the farm-gate scraping over the cobbles jolted her into action. They were back. Hastily she tidied up the scraps of thread and material which littered the room and folded the dress away. If Adam had bought a dress, she didn't want to risk stealing his thunder. She had done what she could for the daughter. Now all she had to do was find the courage to face the father. Cathy made her way downstairs, almost shaking with panic. What could she possibly say to him? What if he didn't mention the previous night at all? What if he treated it all as a big joke? What if...

Her heart sank when she saw Rebecca run off round the side of the house, paper bag in hand, and Adam turn towards the scullery door alone. The warm glow seemed to have turned to cold stone and lay sickeningly on her stomach.

Just be normal; the unfollowable advice spun round in her head. In desperation, as she heard him enter the kitchen, she turned and started to fiddle with the kettle on the stove. If only her heart would stop beating so fast. Words seemed to jump from her lips involuntarily, as if someone had switched on a tape.

'Did you buy much at the shops?' Cathy knew her voice sounded strained and artificial, but she didn't seem to be able to stop. 'Isn't it hot today? It's worse than London. Rebecca looked excited; did you buy her something nice?'

Adam dumped a box of groceries on the table and looked at her. 'A fringed brow-band to keep the flies off Minty's face,' he said evenly. She mustn't look at him. She mustn't catch his eye. Drops of water hissed on the iron hotplate as she jerked the kettle in her nervousness.

'It's too hot for tea, Cathy. Put the kettle down and look at me. I've got things I want to say to you, and they don't involve the weather.'

Only the fear that he would come over, that he would touch her, made Cathy turn slowly and raise her eyes to his face. Even across the width of the room, his gaze seemed to lock on to hers, holding her immobile. She had the sudden fantasy that if he looked upwards she would be swept off her feet, supported by the intensity of the awareness which linked them.

'Last night you said that you loved me. I don't want to waste time playing "let's pretend". If you don't want me, you'll have to tell me. And I won't believe you if you do.'

Despite her nervousness, his arrogance made Cathy smile. She forced herself to walk over to the table and started to unpack the shopping from the box. 'Adam, last night—it was hardly a normal situation. We both got carried away. I can't pretend I don't . . . feel something for you, but what I said before still applies. I can't risk—I don't want to plunge into something and end up getting hurt.'

'And what makes you so sure that holding back will keep you safe? Life is a gamble, Cathy, I told you that before. There are no guarantees that any horse you pick won't fall at the first fence, so you might as well put your money on the one you fancy. And from what you were saying in your cups, I gathered I was favourite.'

His grin caught Cathy off guard and she felt the stiffness inside her thawing as she blushed with embarrassment. Grabbing a lettuce from the box in front of her, she threw it at his chest. 'I was drunk. If you will ply me with champagne at two o'clock in the morning——'

'I thought you said it was just the blood rushing away from your head?' Adam looked at her mockingly, holding the lettuce in front of him like a green bouquet. The incongruity reminded Cathy of another misplaced vegetable, forgotten until now in her rush to finish the dress.

'Did you put a tomato on my bedside-table this morning?'

Her employer swept a bow. 'I had that honour.'

'Why? Or would that be a silly question?'

He raised his eyebrows in mock disdain. 'You mean to say you've never heard of the Language of Vegetables?'

Cathy shook her head, caught up despite herself in his sense of fun.

'It's a dialect of the Language of Flowers. A single red tomato means, "I love you but there aren't any roses in the garden."' Cathy's heart seemed to miss its rhythm. Did he know what he was saying? But his voice was as flippant as ever. 'Plus, I thought that after last night you wouldn't be able to tell the difference for an hour or two, and if you ate it by mistake, at least the vitamin C might do something for your hangover. You did have a hangover, I trust?'

She threw another lettuce, but he fielded it expertly. 'Of course, lettuces are a particularly eloquent vegetable; especially at high speed. That particular one said, "Stop talking nonsense and kiss your housekeeper before she starts on the potatoes." I never disobey a lettuce.'

He made a sudden dart towards her, and Cathy dodged shrieking round the kitchen table. For a few seconds, they faced each other, panting. Adam feinted to the left and she started to circle in the same direction, but while she was still off balance he suddenly vaulted on to the old pine table and pounced. Laughing, kissing and breathing all at once proved difficult, and Cathy's giggles were gradually stifled by the mounting passion of their embrace.

The hours that had passed since he left her in her bedroom might never have existed. His mouth slipped from her lips to her throat and then down to nuzzle the softness of her breasts under her thin shirt, while his strong hands pulled her hips close against the muscled contours of his thighs. At last, breathless, Cathy pulled gently away.

'We have to talk, Adam. Kissing doesn't solve anything.'

'It does if you do it long enough.' He pulled her closer than ever and kissed her again.

It would be so easy to give in, to forget everything except the intoxication of being in his arms. The roughness of his chin rasped gently against her cheek, and her hand went up to stroke his face, revelling in the difference of textures; his maleness against her femininity. Her fingers twined themselves in the dark golden curls at the nape of his neck, pulling him against her as if their bodies would weld together. There was no longer any possibility of pretending that he left her unmoved, but Cathy knew that she no longer cared about her dignity. She loved him; she wanted him with a passion that she had never known was in her. But she had to be sure. Pushing him away was the most difficult thing she had ever done.

'Adam, please! You mustn't bulldoze me like this. I can't think straight when you're kissing me.'

'You can't think straight when I'm not kissing you, you mean. Listen, Cathy, I don't know what's bothering you, but we can sort it out. There aren't any problems we can't handle. Only I don't have time to waste. In three weeks' time, you plan to disappear out of my life. It's you who's forcing the pace, not me. I'm just staking my claim.' He reached into his pocket and brought out a small package. 'I want you to marry me, Cathy. I bought you this.'

Cathy stared blankly at the little square box resting on his palm, and felt the pieces click grimly into place in her head. 'So that's what this is all about. No wonder you were in a hurry. But you might have been a bit more subtle about it, Adam. Surely it could have waited a couple of days?'

'I don't know what you mean.'

'Don't you?' She reached out and took the box, flipping it open with her thumb. The ring inside made her catch her breath involuntarily. Three deep red rubies, flanked with diamonds, on a plain gold band. It was perfect, and she had to fight the desire to slip it on to her finger and see it flame. When Adam Dale decided to acquire a wife, he didn't do things by halves. 'I think you do.'

'No, I don't. I just wanted you to know that I'm serious, Cathy; that I want more than just a casual affair. I want——'

'You want a wife,' she finished for him. 'You want a nice, stable, married background to frighten your ex-wife away from Becca. That's what all this was about, wasn't it? Persuading me to stay.'

'I need you, Cathy. And so does Becca.'

But that's not enough, she wanted to scream at him. 'Do you love me the way you did Mia?' As soon as the words were out, she regretted them. She didn't want to know about Mia...

'No! Mia and I were—it was an enchantment, an intoxication. I think it was almost a kind of madness. We were totally unsuited, and we didn't care. That's not what I feel for you.' Cathy felt jealousy stab at her heart. Wasn't he even going to pretend? She stared bleakly at the floor as he went on. 'I care about you, Cathy. I feel as if I've always known you. You belong here. And it has nothing to do with Mia. I can't deny that marriage would make my claim to custody more secure, but that's not why I'm asking you.'

'Isn't it, Adam? How can you be so sure?'

There was just a fraction too long a delay before he opened his mouth to answer. Cathy shook her head. 'You see? You can't be certain.' Suddenly, she no longer felt angry. 'Oh, Adam—— I understand how you must feel. And I don't blame you; you must be torn apart by worry. I'm not saying that you don't—care for me. And I care about you. But I can't accept this.' She closed the little box and handed it back. Parting from it was a wrench. 'When someone puts a ring like that on my finger, I want to know that it's me he wants to marry. Not just his housekeeper.'

To her surprise, Adam took back the ring without argument. 'I think you're wrong,' he said quietly. 'When I chose this, I wasn't thinking about Mia. I wasn't thinking about anything but the way it would glow against your skin.' He forced a smile. 'But I can't deny that it seemed like the perfect solution. That's the trouble with real life: you have a plot all worked out and then the characters refuse to follow the script.'

He stood silent for a moment, as if expecting her to say something. Cathy didn't dare speak. She had the terrible feeling that, if she opened her mouth, the wrong words would come pouring out: that she would beg him to tell her that he loved her, to lie to her if necessary, to hold her in his arms again and kiss her doubts away. The urge to reach out and touch him was almost overwhelming. Instead, she fixed her gaze on his feet and kept miserably quiet.

At last, he shrugged and slipped the ring-box back into his pocket. 'Well, if I'm to get any work done today, I'd better disappear,' he said lightly. 'I gather my daughter has decided she wants to go to this party tonight.' He looked at Cathy with curiosity. 'Was that anything to do with you? When the invitation came, she told me that she didn't want to go, and yet on the way into town she seemed quite excited about it.'

Cathy smiled nervously. 'It's a secret for the moment, I'm afraid. Will you have time to drive her over, or do you want me to do it?'

'No, I'll do it. Come and disturb me at about six, will you? At least I'll get a couple of hours in before she goes. Then, if you like, I could treat you to a meal at the local pub and we'll pick her up on the way back. It's about time you had an evening off from cooking.'

His matter-of-fact acceptance of the situation seemed to lift a weight from Cathy's shoulders. Thank God he hadn't pushed the advantage he must have known he had over her... If he had kissed her again, she wasn't sure that she would have had the strength to go on resisting. She felt emotionally drained, but she knew she had done the right thing.

So why, as she watched him leave the kitchen, did she feel so empty? And why did her finger ache for a ring it had never worn?

CHAPTER EIGHT

CATHY looked at her creation in delight. The dress was a success. And Rebecca herself, well washed and with her long hair free for once from tangles, and painstakingly brushed into a pale gold cloud, was a character straight out of legend. An Alice, perhaps—but her elfin face was more Fairyland than Wonderland.

'Do I look nice, Cathy?' Rebecca looked shyly at herself in the mirror, twisting and turning to try and see herself from all angles.

'You look beautiful, darling. Like a fairy princess.'

To her surprise, the remark seemed to unsettle the younger girl, who fidgeted on one foot, kicking the other repeatedly against the dresser.

'What's the matter, Becca? You look perfect. Don't you like it?'

'Oh, yes! It's lovely. But . . . what you said—they used to call me that, at school, as a joke. Because once I wrote in a story that my mother was a fairy woman and that's why she didn't live with us any more, only it wasn't supposed to be a story and the teacher said I shouldn't tell lies. But it wasn't really a fib; I only sort of meant it, not really, if you know what I mean. And anyway, Daddy said it was very nearly true. But they called me "Fairy Princess" for ages afterwards, so I wished I hadn't written it.'

A fairy woman. Not a bad description of Mia Tannabrae's ethereal beauty. She felt a stab of unreasoning jealousy that a woman blessed with such looks could have so much else as well—and value it so little. If *she* had had Adam for a husband and Becca for a child... Cathy shook her head at the fiercely protective wave of longing which washed over her, and gently touched Rebecca's hair.

'Well, no one could tease you looking like that,' she smiled. 'You'll be the prettiest girl there, by a long way. Now I'll get dressed up and we'll go and surprise your father. I bet he's never seen you like this before, has he?'

All the time she was dressing, Cathy kept up a flow of conversation, sensing that Rebecca was still very nervous of displaying herself in her finery. Underneath she was fuming at the insensitivity of the teacher in exposing to the ridicule of the class a child whose mother had deserted her. It was hardly surprising that she had created her own fantasies to fill the gap, or that they had spilled over sometimes into 'real life'. Cathy felt tears prickle fiercely at the back of her eyes and blinked them back. Her own involvement frightened her. What was it about this girl and her father that went straight to her heart? She had only known Rebecca a week, and yet already she felt that leaving her would be a betrayal...

'There—how do I look?' She twirled round to show Rebecca her own dress. She would have to

change before they went out, of course—it was too
much for the local pub. But it made a change to
wear a dress again after a week of jeans.

The bright colours suited her, she knew, throwing
her dark colouring into dramatic relief and giving
her a touch of gipsy exoticism. And yet, tonight
there seemed to be something missing... She gazed
in puzzlement at her reflection in the mirror—and
then it came to her. Subconsciously, she had been
looking for a flash of fire on her finger. Her dress
would have been the perfect setting for Adam's
ring. But it was no use wishing. 'Will I do?'

'Aren't you going to undo your hair? You said
you would.'

'Oh, no—I'd rather not, Rebecca. I'm not going
to the party; I'd just have to do it all up again
afterwards.'

The younger girl pouted. 'But you promised you
would dress up properly. It's nicer like that. And
Daddy likes it.'

Which was exactly the problem, thought Cathy
as she reluctantly let Rebecca remove the hairpins
that held it precariously under control. If only she
knew what she wanted; if only she could be sure
that his feelings for her were prompted by more
than convenience and sexual attraction. It had all
seemed so simple before. Now she was torn. She
was convinced that their relationship had no future,
and yet she wanted nothing more than to feel his
touch again. She found the thought of him seeing
her dressed like this strangely exciting—but part of
her shrank from the display.

She brushed her hair through and tossed it back from her face. 'Come on, then, Cinderella, let's go and give your dad a shock. He won't know what's hit him.' Feeling almost as nervous as Rebecca had been before, she led the way downstairs.

Gesturing to Rebecca to keep quiet, Cathy knocked twice on the heavy door of the study. The typewriter keys paused momentarily and they heard Adam's voice, preoccupied, call back 'Five minutes!' before the tapping resumed. Cathy felt Rebecca pulling her away from the door, but having once plucked up her courage she was in no mood to creep quietly away. Who did Adam think he was, anyway? Didn't his daughter deserve some of his attention? Cathy took a deep breath and walked into the room.

It was almost funny to watch the emotions chasing each other over Adam's face. Surprise and then anger at being disturbed, superseded almost immediately by amazement at the difference in her appearance and frank enjoyment—finally settling into mild embarrassment that she had misunderstood the nature of the evening's entertainment ahead of them. Cathy stepped in before he could start to explain her mistake.

'It's not me you're supposed to be staring at—I'm just the fairy godmother.' She looked round but Rebecca was still hiding outside in the hallway. She reached outside to beckon her in.

Rebecca's nervousness had touched her normally pale cheeks with pink and her eyes glistened. She entered the room as if it were a stage and she were

making her entrance as a woman. Cathy was suddenly aware of her as an equal, not a child, and
even felt a momentary pang of anguish in the
presence of a natural beauty far beyond anything
she could ever hope to attain. Then she turned her
attention back to Adam—and realised that she had
made a terrible mistake.

This time his expression wasn't funny. His face
was sickly yellow under his tan, as if the blood had
been drained out of it, and his mouth moved
soundlessly. He stared at his daughter, not with the
amused delight that Cathy had foreseen, but with
horror and—inexplicably—a fleeting look of
something like hatred. For two seconds that seemed
like hours, the tension held, to be broken by father
and daughter together as Rebecca let out a wail and
rushed from the room and Adam stood up abruptly,
knocking his chair backwards on to the flagged
floor.

'What is it with you women? Why can't you leave
her alone?' The venomous fury in his voice made
Cathy back towards the door, half afraid that he
might strike her. 'It's like foot-binding in China—
it was the women who wouldn't give it up. Each
generation warping and crippling the next as they
were twisted themselves. I thought you were different, but you're just like the rest of them. You
couldn't bear to see her growing up naturally. You
had to turn her into a whore like her mother.'

The ugliness of his words jolted Cathy into response. 'How dare you talk about your daughter
like that—or me?' She was almost hissing the words

in an effort to keep the volume down. If only Rebecca had gone far enough out of earshot! 'What's the matter with you, anyway, Adam? You're not making any kind of sense—and think what you've done to Rebecca. She was lovely and she knew it—and you've kicked her in the teeth.'

'Oh, yes, she knew it all right. I could see it in her eyes. And she liked it, didn't she? Does it make you proud to know that you've opened Pandora's box? That you were the first to give her the fix? I thought you were a sensible woman, God help me, or I would have kept you away from her. Why couldn't you leave the poor child alone?'

The pain in his voice overtook the anger, and his face seemed to shrink into tiredness, but Cathy was too angry herself now to feel any pity. 'I didn't leave the poor child alone, Adam, because she was crying in the night over that damn party. She didn't dare go because she had nothing to wear which wouldn't be laughed at. You're so busy cosseting a thirteen-year-old grudge against her mother that you can't see what's in front of your eyes. She's growing up, you selfish bastard, and she's going to be a beautiful woman whether you give her permission or not. All you can do is make sure that she feels as bad about it as possible, and you're certainly going the right way about that.

'All right, so her mother left you. Maybe she really was as much of a monster as you've built her up to be—or perhaps not. I don't know and I don't want to. But Becca is only her daughter, not her reincarnation. She's a person in her own right and she's got as much of you in her as of her mother.'

Adam's fists were clenching and unclenching and his face was white—whether with anger or shock at her words, Cathy wasn't sure. But she couldn't stop, the bitter words propelled by a sick feeling of betrayal not only for Rebecca but for her own foolish hopes. How could she ever have deluded herself into believing that this man might have some real feeling for her? His emotions were still tied to the woman who had bewitched him thirteen years before. 'If you ask me, she's worth more than either of you. And I just hope to God that she was crying loudly enough not to hear her father call her a whore. You're not fit to look after a child—I'm not even sure you're sane!'

She didn't wait to see the effect of her speech but turned, half blinded by furious tears, and pushed out of the room. It was all her fault, that was the terrible thing. Rebecca had known what her father's reaction would be, but she had persuaded her it would be all right. Goodness knew what damage had been done. She had to find her and try to help her understand.

But Rebecca wasn't in her room—only the dress, stuffed ignominiously in the waste-paper basket, showed that she had been there. Cathy ran to the window and looked out over the field at the back of the farmhouse. Yes, there she was. A small figure in jeans, staggering under the weight of saddle and bridle as it advanced on the sturdy Dales pony tethered to the gate.

'Rebecca!' But, although the child must have heard, there was no response. It was no use. She knew as she rushed downstairs and outside, stumbling in her high heels on the cobbles of the yard, that there was no chance of catching up with Minty and his rider. By the time she reached the paddock they were climbing the steep path up to the fell.

Cathy called again, but the only answer was her own voice, echoing back from the slope in the hot, still air. Perhaps Rebecca had the best idea, anyway—they all needed to cool off. Although in this heat it seemed scarcely possible; there was no breath of wind and the atmosphere felt as close and heavy as her own anger. She looked longingly at the rocky heights above her. Perhaps up there there would be a breeze. A walk would do her good.

Her first step on to the soft turf reminded her that she wasn't exactly dressed for fell-climbing. She would have to change—but the last thing she wanted now was to go back inside and risk meeting Adam again. It was difficult to know which would be worse: his continued anger or his apologies. On impulse she kicked off the elegant shoes she had worn to go with her dress and wriggled her toes in the grass. It was delightfully cool between her toes. Well, why not? She needn't go very far, and the ground was soft to walk on. She hung her shoes on the gate-post and set off up the path.

The first clap of thunder took Cathy by surprise, but immediately she wondered why she hadn't expected it. The weather had been so unbearably close all day—a storm would clear the air. But it would ruin her dress. Dark clouds rolled in quickly, casting a dark shadow over the valley and hills. Looking back down the fell, the farm was nowhere in sight, hidden by the slopes below.

Which way would be best? It ought to be possible to cut diagonally down the hill, almost halving the distance. A warm heavy splash of rain decided her. There did seem to be some sort of path leading down. Her feet slithered on the already wet grass as she set off down across the slope.

Ten minutes later, she was soaked through and the path had degenerated into no more than a sheep track. Worse, it had looped round and, unless she had lost her sense of direction, no longer headed in the direction of the farm. It was difficult to be sure. The sky now was dark as night and the rain whipped down fiercely, forcing her to keep her face tucked down and making it difficult to see.

She would have to seek shelter here on the hill until the violence diminished. Back near where she had turned off the main track there had been the remains of an old sheepfold. That would have to do.

Before she had gone more than half the distance, Cathy found her path blocked by a stream. It wasn't a very wide stream—she could have jumped over it without much effort. But she hadn't passed it on the way down. Shivering now, as the wind which had come with the rain cut through her wet clothing, Cathy turned to retrace her steps, looking out for a turning that she might have missed. But there was nothing; or if there was, the darkness obscured it.

Her eyes, straining in the gloom, began to see strange shapes and humps just out of the range of clear vision. The storm rolled inexorably nearer, the thunder exploding like a dynamite charge every few minutes and the lightning crackling though the sky, its brilliant illumination making it even more difficult to see clearly in the murky darkness that followed.

She was back at the stream again, the narrow trickle now noticeably swollen with the rain. She would have to paddle if she wanted to cross it now—but what was the point? All she knew was that she was lost. If she crossed it she would only wander further and further from the area she knew. At least here she had some chance of correcting her mistake when the storm died down.

But there was no shelter, and the ground was wet and sodden. She couldn't just sit and wait; at least if she kept walking it would help to keep her warm. And she felt strangely reluctant to leave the little stream. The only fixed feature on this unknown landscape, its nearness gave her a sense of security that she was loath to give up.

She decided to follow it for a while. At worst, she would just have to retrace her steps when visibility improved, but there was always the chance that she might come across some shelter. Or the stream might even join on to the beck that flowed down beside the farm. At least with it flowing beside her she couldn't become any more hopelessly lost. She started to follow it cautiously down the hill.

At last the storm seemed to spend its force and roll on towards the next valley. The rain gradually petered out, but the sky remained as gloomy as ever. And her ears seemed to have become attuned to the driving of wind and water; she could still seem to hear a rushing sound, even though the droplets no longer fell.

Cathy shook her head to clear it and stumbled on. Surely she must be nearly down in the valley by now? The rushing sound gradually increased in volume—and its significance suddenly flashed into her mind like a bolt of lightning, paralysing her with fear.

It wasn't an hallucination. The sound was real, and coming nearer. Not rain, but a different sort of falling water. A waterfall—and she had nearly walked right over the edge. She sat down on the soaked grass, trembling with awareness of her danger. If the rain hadn't stopped she would have followed her bubbling lifeline right over the edge of a crag.

Adam's words came back to her. 'Don't go wandering up to the head of the valley without a guide...limestone country...riddled with potholes.' Could she possibly have strayed that far? It was difficult to believe, but then, until the rain had started, she hadn't been paying much attention to time or distance.

Cathy realised that she was now shaking uncontrollably, from cold and horror. To fall over a cliff, to die or be injured and lie in pain waiting for rescue—that was bad enough. But to fall down a pot-hole was the stuff of nightmares. If she had survived the fall, what chance would there have been of rescue? She would have been invisible; left in the dark to die of injury or exposure; her last view of the world a circle of light far above her head.

She knew now that she didn't dare move another foot until daylight returned. It was summer—surely she wouldn't die of exposure in summer? But better that than to lie bleeding in the dark. Curling up on the wet ground, she tried to forget the cold that seemed to be creeping right into the marrow of her bones.

She was awakened by something warm and moist against her waxy skin, and an unpleasantly fetid breath puffing into her face. Cathy felt confused rather than startled by this unusual awakening. Why didn't they leave her alone? It wasn't time to get up yet; it was still dark outside. And they had pulled the covers off her; she was so cold.

She pushed the face away and heard it whine, then bark sharply. Why had they let the dog into her room? She tried to tell it to be quiet, but the words seemed to get jumbled up. Perhaps if she ignored them they would go away. She felt around for the covers. Wet. The bed was wet. Perhaps she should get up, but she was so sleepy. It could wait until morning. Cathy drifted back into the dream she had been enjoying so much. A dream of warmth.

But they wouldn't let her enjoy her dream. He was picking her up, shaking her, shouting at her. Perhaps he was angry because the bed was wet. She tried to explain that it wasn't her fault, but he didn't seem to understand.

Why didn't he let her sleep? She could feel him fumbling behind her back, pulling at the zip of her dress. He was trying to rape her! Cathy hit out wildly and felt her fist connect with something hard. He swore and held her close to him, pulling the dress roughly down from her shoulders and down over her hips. Then he swept her up into his arms. The sudden movement made Cathy feel dizzy and sick. Then the darkness claimed her and she slipped back into the dream.

Returning to consciousness was like swimming up from the bottom of a deep, dark lake. At first there was only darkness, then small flashes started to filter through to mingle with her dreams. Someone was touching her, stroking her as if she was a cat. She was a cat. It was warm and sensuous and she arched against the hand, purring.

She could hardly move. She was somewhere small, very tight. Her cheek was pressed against something warm and rough and somehow soft and hard at the same time. The pot-hole! She was trapped in one of the underground tunnels! Panicky and gasping for air, she broke surface and opened her eyes.

'Thank God.' The words rumbled against her cheek; reaching her as much by touch as by hearing. The darkness was suddenly pierced by a blinding light, shining on her face. She moved slightly and tried to focus her vision. The rough warm wall she had felt in her dream was a man's chest, naked. The voice had been Adam's. She was still aware of the constriction around her. What was going on?

'Adam?' She felt his arms round her tighten, pulling the rough wool against her skin. Wool. Where was her dress? What was she wearing? 'Adam, where are we? What's happening?' She pushed him away and tried to sit up, but it was impossible. Something held her down.

The light went out and he held her close, quietening her struggles. 'It's all right, Cathy. You got yourself lost on the hill in the rain, so I came to find you. You're safe now. We'll have to stay here until it's light enough to see, and then I'll take you home.'

She lay quietly in his arms, trying to piece things together. The storm; yes, she remembered that now. And following the stream. And then the water-fall—she clung to the hard body beside her for re-assurance as the terror swept over her again. 'I nearly walked over the edge. I was following the stream...'

His arms tightened round her. 'You certainly managed to pick the wrong place for walking in the dark. Didn't you realise there was a storm brewing?

Luckily, Becca saw you walking along the ridge just before it started, so when you didn't come back I knew where to start looking.'

Suddenly he was holding her so tightly that she could hardly breathe. 'Oh, Cathy, I thought I'd lost you. I'd never have forgiven myself if anything had happened to you. I know I can't wipe out the things I said to you this afternoon. But when Becca walked through that door—it was like seeing her mother's ghost come back to haunt me. I was irrational, and God knows, I've hurt both of you. But I'm sorry. I've tried to explain to Becca and I think perhaps she understands. Can you try and forgive me?'

Oh, yes, the argument, of course. Cathy realised that she had forgotten all about the scene in his study. Things were beginning to fall into place. They were still out on the fell; and the tightness around them was a sleeping-bag. But there were other memories, too. Struggling with him, her dress being torn off—and now Adam lying naked beside her. But the rest was blank. If only she could see his face. Surely she would remember if...?

'Adam, what happened when you found me?' Hesitantly she touched his chest, and felt something inside her stir as her fingers contacted the crisp golden hair which covered it. 'Why are you—where are your clothes?'

Even in the darkness, somehow she could feel him smile. 'You're wearing most of them,' he said. 'Although you didn't much like the idea at the time. You seemed to be under the impression that my designs were less than honourable—and I have a feeling that you've given me quite a professional black eye for my trouble.' He stroked his hand down her back and Cathy shivered as the rough wool scratched her skin. 'You were in quite a bad way, you know—half-delirious with exposure. Just at the hostile, obstreperous stage. But don't worry, I told you before that when I make love to you, I intend to make sure you'll remember it in the morning.'

Cathy blushed, turning her face away as if he would see it through the darkness. He was assuming so much. And yet his quiet assurance was somehow deeply comforting, like his arms around her and the firm wall of his chest crushed against her by the tight embrace of the sleeping-bag. This was real; this was the world. Her worries seemed insubstantial by comparison.

She buried her face in his chest, breathing in the warm scent of his body, and felt him respond, catching his breath and running his hands down to rest on her hips, pulling her against him. His legs were bare; she could feel his hard shin with her foot.

'Are you...am I wearing all your clothes?' Cathy's voice sounded different to her own ears; thicker, heavier. She blushed again at her question, but she had to know. The thought that he was completely naked beside her... Excitement rose in her throat, almost blotting out the knowledge of their surroundings.

'I used my shirt to dry you. And I kept my shorts, for decency's sake.' He moved against her and, hardly realising what she was doing, her hands went to his buttocks, feeling the tense muscle beneath the thin cotton fabric. He nuzzled her hair as he went on. 'But that could be easily remedied.' His hand went down and somehow hooked the shorts from under her fingers. The sleeping-bag rippled and her hand lay, not on smooth cotton, but on warm flesh.

Then his hand was moving up under the woollen jersey, touching her, caressing her, moving closer and closer to her breasts. Cathy felt her entire being concentrated in those sensitive, longing peaks. She wanted his touch more than she had ever wanted anything in her life; all other thoughts were obliterated by that surging desire. He swept his hands over every other inch of her under the harsh wool, sensitising it, awakening it. She burned, and still he didn't touch them, cold peaks of ice above the raging fire.

'Oh, please, please.' Her need made her shameless, and when he pulled the oiled wool up, exposing her, she arched her body to meet his mouth as it descended. A shudder ran though her frame as the warm softness of his lips and gently caressing tongue melted the ice, teasing a moan of pleasure from deep in her throat. He moved from one soft, rounded breast to the other, filling the void his caresses had created. His hands slipped downwards, under the loose waistband of the borrowed jeans on to the flat plateau of her stomach and round to grip the round softness of her buttocks, kneading them like dough in his strong hands.

She raised her hips and he pushed the heavy denim down her legs, pulling it with his feet when he could no longer reach with his hands, forcing it down to the bottom of the sleeping-bag. Her body was naked against his in the damp warmth of the sleeping-bag, and she almost screamed at the intimacy of that first total contact, flesh against flesh. His voice was ragged and thick with desire. 'Oh, Cathy—I want you so much. I was so afraid... Oh, God, please let me love you.'

In answer, she pulled him against her with all her strength, as if her body could merge into his. She didn't trust herself to speak above a whisper. 'I love you, Adam. I want you to make love to me. And I promise I won't forget it by the morning.'

CHAPTER NINE

'DON'T go to sleep, Cathy. Talk to me. I don't want to risk you getting cold again.'

It seemed impossible that she would ever be cold: her whole body glowed with inner warmth. All her doubts seemed to have melted away in the heat of their loving. It was as if she had finally found the piece that made sense of the whole jigsaw; the key to the door of the secret garden. She lay cradled with her head on Adam's crooked arm, feeling the rhythm of his breathing and the beating of his heart. She was so——

'Wake up, my love. Only an hour or so to go now. You can sleep when we get home. This is the coldest part of the night—try to stay awake. What would you like to talk about?'

'I don't know,' she said dreamily. 'I love you, Adam. I hadn't realised it would be so beautiful.'

He hugged her fiercely. 'You should have told me it was your first time. I could have waited. This is hardly the ideal situation——'

She reached up and kissed him on the lips, cuddling close. 'It was perfect, nothing could be better than that. I needed you so much. And I'm unlikely to forget it—isn't that what you wanted?'

She could replay the memory in such intensity that it was as if it was all happening again. The burning need, the momentary pain, and the look of shock and tenderness on her lover's face when he realised; and then the gradually building tide of sensation, wave upon wave of pleasure until at last every nerve-ending in her body seemed to ignite with cold fire and she heard her own voice cry out. And then, when she thought she was spent, to feel his quickening movements push her on past the barrier until they both dissolved together in a mutual release that left her weak and light-headed. Light-bodied, too; she felt she was floating on a cushion of air——

He was shaking her again. 'I'm sorry, Cathy, but you must stay awake. Maybe we should play a game?'

'How about I-Spy?' She giggled. 'I spy with my little eye something beginning with "D". Give up? "Dark". Your turn.'

'Nitwit.' He nibbled her ear. 'How about I-Feel? Much more interesting and appropriate. I feel with my little finger something beginning with——'

Her squeal woke the old dog that lay patiently beside her master, and Betsy padded over anxiously to sniff at Cathy's face. 'Now look what you've done—I can almost hear her poor joints creaking. Why don't you tell me a story? Pretend I'm Becca. Tell me about the Seal Wife.'

'Did she tell you about that? It was always one of her favourites—I don't know why. It's very sad. It was one of the tales I heard from my Highland grandmother, and I've always regretted that I never thought to tape her telling them. She had the exact words passed down to her from her mother, and she from hers. They were probably hundreds of years old.'

'Don't you know the words, then?'

'Not really; just a few phrases that come back to me. But I can remember the stories.'

'Tell me.' Cathy settled herself to listen, looking up at his face. There was just enough light to make out the shape of his mouth and the dark-on-darkness of his eyes. Above them clouds scudded across the sky, only visible as they obscured the faint glow of the stars.

'Once upon a time, in the islands beyond the sunset, there was a fisherman who sailed further than the rest to search for the herring. And one day when he was searching, he saw the grey seals playing in the water ahead of him and so he followed them, for he knew they would be knowing where the herring swam. And at last he came to a great shoal, so thick that the water gleamed like a pile of silver pieces.

'And he threw in his nets and took a catch that filled his boat to the gunwales. But when he pulled in the net for the third and last time, the weight in it was not of fish. At first he thought that he had caught a seal, and made ready with his knife to kill it for the fat. Then the light changed and he saw that it was not a seal but a woman, as beautiful as the moonlight on the water. And he loved her from that moment.'

Adam's voice had taken on a sing-song, dreamlike quality. Cathy felt surrounded by the magic of the simple story; utterly content.

'And she saw the knife and was afraid and begged him to spare her life, saying that she would be wife to him and bear him a child. So he threw back the herring that he had caught and brought her into the boat and took her back to the shore to be his wife. And for many months they lived happily together. But now, this was the way of it; every night after he was asleep she would rise up from the bed and leave the croft and return in the morning early with her hair wet and twined with weed. But when he questioned her, she bade him be silent. And because she was beautiful, and a good wife to him, he asked her no more.

'And at length she bore him a son. But the women of the village whispered that no good would come of the marriage, for no man had ever taken to him one of the fairy kind and come away unscathed. And they knew by the manner of her finding that this was no mortal woman. So they mocked him, saying that at night she went to her fairy lover and that he was no man to allow it. And at last, he stayed awake one night and followed his wife where she went. He saw her go to the seashore and raise a certain rock and take out a seal skin, and put it on. And there was no longer a woman on the shore, but only a grey seal swimming.

'Cold, he waited on the beach until the dawn turned white in the sky. And at last he saw the seal wife emerge from the waves and go to the rock, as beautiful as when he first saw her. And he loved her, but his heart was cold in him to think that she might leave him. So he lifted the rock and took the sealskin and hid it in the barn beneath the fleeces and said nothing, but only waited.

'And the first night, his wife left the bed but returned before the dawn, weeping. And the second night the same. Then on the third, she went no more to the shore but stayed in her bed. And the man was glad. But the seal wife wept day and night and would not be comforted, and her beauty melted away like sea-foam on the sand. And at last the man could bear it no more and he fetched the seal skin from under the fleeces and gave it to her, saying, "My heart was cold with the fear that you might leave me, so I hid the skin, because I love you."

'And she took the skin and wept again. And she kissed her child and gave him to the man and said, "I would have stayed with you willingly and been wife to you and mother to our son. But now I must go back to the sea or die." And she left him and went down to the shore and never more returned.

'And the man took to him a wife of mortal kind, to mother the child, and he loved her after the way of men. But at night he would leave their bed and stand on the shore, watching the moonlight on the water and calling for his lost seal wife.'

There was a long silence. Cathy felt the warmth inside her shrivel; the flame flicker and go out. How could he not see it? How could his daughter know him so well and he himself not at all? Tears welled up in her eyes and trickled down her cheeks, wetting his chest.

'What——?' Adam put out a finger and touched her cheek. 'Cathy, love, don't cry. You're as bad as Becca—she used to cry every time at that one, but she always asked for it again. It's only a story.'

'Is it, Adam? Becca didn't think so, and neither do I.'

'What do you mean? You're not making sense. Of course it's just a story. North Sea fishing statistics show a remarkably low incidence of seal wives recently.' He kissed her on the top of the head and pulled her against him. 'Never mind, my little addle-pate. It's nearly dawn. We'll be able to leave in half an hour or so.'

'Don't laugh at me, Adam.' It was so warm in his arms, so comforting. But she couldn't forget the wistful grief in his voice as he came to his story's conclusion. 'Becca told me that she was told off at school once for writing that her mother was a fairy woman—and that you said it was very nearly true.'

'Did I say that? I suppose I might have done; I remember the occasion. That thick-skinned teacher of theirs set the class to write about "My Mother" without even thinking about the effect on a child that didn't have one. And then she had the cheek to tell me that Becca had to learn the distinction between fact and fantasy. I told her that I had made a very good living by confusing the two, and I didn't intend to risk stifling my daughter's imagination. Anyway, in a way Becca was right.'

His voice hardened. 'Mia was the nearest thing to a fairy woman that I've ever met or hope to meet. Beautiful, enchanting, totally selfish and light-heartedly cruel. Fairies aren't the pretty little things they're made out to be in Victorian children's books, you know.'

'I know. "No man had ever taken to him one of the fairy kind and come away unscathed." That's you, Adam, though you may not consciously admit it. But I heard it in your voice as you told the story—and so did Becca.'

'Cathy...' There was real concern in his voice now, and in the gradually increasing light she could see it reflected on his face. 'You aren't really upset about this, are you? I loved Mia; I was bowled over when she left, I admit that. But it's been thirteen years. I love you now—I want to marry you. She's nothing to me.'

'Isn't she? You love me, you say, and your daughter, and yet you practically tear us to pieces because I dress Rebecca in a way that reminds you of her. You said it was like seeing a ghost, but it was a ghost created out of your own feelings. I saw your face, remember, and the pain and grief on it wasn't thirteen years old. It was very much alive. Maybe you do love me, in a way. But your grandmother never told you how the mortal wife felt, when her husband spent the nights calling to the seals.'

'Cathy, stop this.' He slid to a sitting position and Cathy felt him shiver as the cool morning air touched his naked skin. 'You're overwrought and imagining things. Whatever I did or didn't feel for Mia has nothing to do with us now. I want to marry you—I thought we'd settled that. I'm prepared to wait until you're ready, but I'll never let you go. Not now. You had me doubting myself, but not any more. Didn't last night prove anything to you?'

'"And the man took to him a wife of mortal kind, to mother the child and he loved her after the way of men."' Cathy's face felt stiff and frozen as she forced out the words. 'That's not enough for me, Adam. I do love you and I believe you feel something for me. But I won't spend the rest of my life competing with a ghost. I'm sorry. You'd better take me back.'

'You're damn right I'm going to take you back. I'm not listening to anything you say until you've had a hot bath and about twenty-four hours' sleep. And if you think I'm going to let you go because of some half-baked Celtic fairytale, you'd better think again.' He pulled himself out of the sleeping-bag and stood up, magnificently naked in the grey morning light.

Cathy felt desire stirring in her again as the sight of him re-awakened all her memories of the previous night. How could she resist him? But at the same time she knew that she had to be strong, all the more so because of the power he held over her. There was no safety with a man like that, even without the spell Mia Tannabrae had laid on him. She should have followed her instincts and kept well away.

Silently resolving to leave the farm as soon as she could, Cathy handed him his jeans and shirt, pulled up from the depths of the sleeping-bag. Fumbling around under its cover, she pulled on his shorts under the woollen jersey that she still wore. Her ruined dress lay in a sodden heap on the grass. Like her hopes.

'Stay there.' He reached down as she started to wriggle out of the padded cocoon and pushed her back into its warmth. 'You can't walk back dressed like that. The rain may have stopped but it's still what the locals call a ''lazy wind''—it can't be bothered to blow round you so it blows straight through.'

'But you can't leave me here!' The fear that she had almost forgotten came surging back and, ignoring his protest, Cathy struggled out and stood up. It was unreasonable, of course. It was light now, and he knew where she was...but, all the same, she knew that she would rather crawl back to the farm than lie there alone and wait.

'Idiot.' The word was affectionate, but Cathy could feel her panic rising. He didn't—couldn't—understand. She watched him loop a heavy coil of rope around his body and adjust it for comfort. Rope. So her fears had been well founded. He had half expected to find her at the bottom of a cliff, or a pot-hole. If the rain hadn't stopped... Cathy suddenly realised that the morning was silent. Unnaturally so. There was no sound of the waterfall which had so nearly claimed her, nor of the brook which had been her treacherous guide. Had she imagined the whole thing? The memory was so vivid, so real. If he left it might come back——

'Adam.' It was difficult even to ask the question. 'Adam, I followed a stream last night, and I could hear a waterfall. Why can't I hear them now? Surely it can't all have been a dream? The stream was just there...' Her voice petered out as she made the gesture. There was nothing but the coarse moorland grass, wet with dew. No sound but a distant curlew—and Adam's laughter.

He was laughing at her! She spun back to face him and some of her feelings must have shown on her face because she found herself being hugged tightly against his damp shirt. 'I'm sorry, Cathy, don't worry. You weren't hallucinating. It's just one of the tricks this country plays on people daft enough to wander round in the dark. Look.' He led her down the slope, holding her firmly against him with one arm wrapped round her waist. Cathy knew she ought to push him away, but her legs and arms felt weak and she was glad of the support. Then something happened that made her cling to him desperately, limp with fear and simultaneous relief.

Quite suddenly, the ground seemed to drop away in front of them into a deep, ragged-edged hole, as if the earth were an apple cored by a giant cook. Near the top, small plants clung to the crevices in the rocks. Below, all was dark. There was a slow drip-dripping of water into the depths.

'Horseman's Pot.' His deep voice seemed to swirl down into the darkness. 'That was your waterfall.

That stream you followed was real enough, and this is where it finished up. Where you would have finished, too, if you hadn't stopped when you did.'

'But where has it gone?'

'Into the rock. This country is limestone, porous rock. That's why there are so few streams in summer; the water soaks right in. It's only in real storms like last night that the ground becomes water-logged and then the becks start to flow. You won't see your stream again until the next thunderstorm.'

Cathy heard his words, but distantly, as if from the bottom of a deep shaft. She was staring down into the darkness and then her vision seemed to telescope. It was as if she were looking up; up to a point of light that was Adam and life. And his voice was fading away.

She swayed forwards and felt his grip tighten, dragging her back. 'Just because I brought the rope doesn't mean I want to use it, you know. I think we should leave the pot-holing for another day. Come on, my little lemming—let's get you home.'

'Don't leave me here, Adam—I can walk.' The hole was behind them now as they made their way up the slope, but Cathy had the feeling that it was lurking at the back of her mind, to swallow her into its blackness if he left her alone.

'You don't need to walk. I'm going to carry you. Come on, back in the sleeping-bag and let's make a start. I told Becca to call the Fell Rescue if we weren't back by six.' Ignoring her protests, he bundled her back into the bag and picked her up.

'I'll have to walk slowly for Betsy, anyway. Last night I think she sensed the urgency and was rushing around like a puppy, but I'm afraid it's catching up with her now.'

The pace he set didn't seem so very slow to Cathy as she jogged uncomfortably with every step over the uneven turf. She held herself stiffly, afraid that to relax against him would be the beginning of the end of her resolve. Luckily, he didn't try to talk. She tried to work out what route they were taking, but it looked unfamiliar, even allowing for her un-usual angle of perspective. It was obviously a short-cut. In less than a hour, he was unhooking the farm gate with his elbow and carrying her through, then depositing her in the porch while he fumbled for his keys.

Home at last. Cathy recoiled as the thought slipped unbidden into her mind. Since when had this been home? The sooner she could make a clean break, the better. Pushing Adam's proffered help aside, she let her wrappings drop and stood shakily on the flagged floor.

'I can manage.' Then, shamed by his hurt expression, she went on in a softer tone, 'I'll just go up to bed, I think. You'd better go and tell Becca you're back; she'll be worried sick.'

But as she spoke Rebecca's tousled head peered down through the wooden banisters. Her face was white and there were dark smudges under the china-blue eyes.

'I'm glad Daddy found you,' she said, in an odd monotone. 'I knew he would. And Betsy had to go, didn't she, to sniff you out? Like a lamb in the snow.'

Her father saw through her at once. Dropping the coil of rope, he bounded up the stairs three at a time and knelt down to crush her in his arms. 'Oh, Becca, I'm sorry. You were all alone, I know and you must have been scared. But I couldn't have found Cathy without Betsy's help. It's all right now, darling; we're back. And I promise I won't leave you like that again.'

Father and daughter clung silently together. Cathy felt a pang of envy at their togetherness, feeling excluded and very much alone. But, as if Adam had read her mind, his next words pulled her back into their warm circle. 'Becca, why don't you and Cathy go and catch up on your sleep? You could both go in my bed if you like.' He looked up at Cathy, his eyes pleading for her co-operation. She nodded. She could hardly refuse—and besides, she had a childishly urgent need not to be alone.

'Come on, Becca. I'm still awfully cold. You can be my hot-water bottle.' The heat of the child's warm hand in her own made her realise just how true that was. Suddenly there was nothing more important than falling into a warm bed. Three minutes later, one arm thrown protectively across the younger girl's waist, she was asleep.

CHAPTER TEN

'WHAT the hell do you think you're doing?' His voice cut through the air like a whip. Cathy started guiltily, jumping in front of her open case in a futile attempt to conceal it. 'No, don't bother to answer that. I can see for myself. You're packing. Would it be too much to ask why?'

She took a deep breath before she dared reply. If only Adam had remained closeted in his study all morning as usual. What instinct had made him change his routine? It wasn't going to be easy to stand firm in the face of his anger—and she felt dangerously close to the end of her strength already. The twenty-four hours that had passed since her ordeal on the moor had only dulled the edge of her exhaustion. 'It's better if I go back to London, Adam,' she said unsteadily. 'My staying here isn't fair on either of us. I've arranged for Sally to pull someone in from another job as a replacement.'

'I don't want a replacement. I want you.'

'She's not like the others—Mary MacIver is one of the best I've got. She's a lovely woman; Becca will like her, I promise.'

'Becca *loves* you.' He emphasised the word with quiet savagery. 'And you promised her you'd stay. Have you forgotten that already—along with everything else?' Pain mingled with the anger in his

voice. 'What about the other night, Cathy? Have
you forgotten that as well?'

'I haven't forgotten.' She would never forget it:
that first touch of his body, naked and heavy on
hers in the tight warmth of the sleeping-bag; the
searing ecstasy of their lovemaking. But nor could
she ever remember it now without the bitter disil-
lusionment of realising that she would never fill the
central space in his heart that he filled in hers. No
relationship, however physically fulfilling, could
survive that sort of basic inequality. 'That's why I
have to go.'

'Don't be so damned melodramatic. What do you
think I'm going to do? Tie you to the bed and rape
you? We're both adults, Cathy—or at least I
suppose we are. If you want to go back to your
precious professional relationship, I won't stop you.
Just because you won't sleep with me doesn't mean
you can't do the job I'm paying you for. Don't
forget you took my money in advance.' The delib-
erate brutality of his words was like a slap in the
face. Cathy was almost glad of it. Anger was easier
to handle than the pity she had begun to feel.

'I'll pay you back,' she flung defiantly. 'Every
penny.' Oh, God, what had possessed her to say
that? Sally would have drawn her salary by now,
and the adverts would have gone out. She'd have
to cash some of her savings certificates; the agency
account would be bare.

'I don't want your money; I want the services I
paid for. You signed a contract.'

'Then sue me!' she flared. 'Our agreement was that I would stay so long as you behaved.'

'Behaved?' For a moment, she thought he was going to hit her. 'Is that how you class what happened between us then? Misbehaviour?'

'Yes—no—oh, Adam, please don't let's part like this.' Her anger evaporated, leaving her on the verge of tears. 'I have to get away, to sort out my feelings——'

'I don't give a damn about your feelings! Try thinking about someone else for a change, Cathy. I've just had another call from my solicitor; Mia has set the wheels in motion. She's definitely making a claim for custody. I need you more than ever now, Cathy; you can't just walk away.'

Cathy felt her resolve strengthened by his harshness. He was no longer even keeping up the pretence of disinterest. 'I'm sorry, Adam, but I've made up my mind. You'll have your "stable background". Mrs MacIver has agreed to a three-month contract—that's far longer than I could have stayed. And she'll be here by Friday.'

'Oh, no, she won't. You're staying here, whether you like it or not. If you think I'm going to drive you to the station——'

'I've ordered a taxi,' she said tiredly. If only he would give up and leave her alone. 'You can't kidnap me, Adam. This is Yorkshire, not the China Seas. There's nothing you can do.'

'No?' He swung round and stalked out of the room. His air of grim determination filled Cathy with foreboding—but, after all, what could he do?

Sally had strict instructions not to allow him to interfere with their plans. Hurriedly, she bundled the rest of her clothes into the suitcase. The taxi would be arriving any minute. And, just in case Adam decided to forbid it entrance, she decided to go and wait for it in the lane.

He was leaning on the gate, watching her. Cathy could feel his eyes boring into her. For the fifth time in as many minutes, she looked despairingly at her watch, silently begging the hands to move faster. She had to get away...

'It won't be coming. I cancelled it.'

'What? But it was on its way...' Cathy stared at him aghast.

'Radio control,' he explained succinctly. He was proud of having outwitted her! Didn't he realise what he was doing to her? Or was it just that he didn't care? 'And I explained that it was my daughter playing practical jokes,' he went on, 'so don't bother trying to rebook. Why don't you just accept that you're staying?'

'Because I'm not.' He wasn't the only one who could think ahead. 'Sally is expecting me. If I don't turn up, she'll start causing a fuss. How much good will it do you to be spread across the papers for holding me against my will?'

Adam's eyes narrowed. 'You—you're bluffing. You wouldn't do that to Becca... Phone her and tell her you've changed your plans.'

She held his gaze, her jaw firm and set, praying that he wouldn't realise how close she was to breakdown. 'No. I told you, Adam, I'm not staying under the same roof as you another day.'

He clenched his fist and seemed about to explode with fury—but the eruption never took place. He gave the smallest of shrugs and seemed to force himself to relax, although underneath she could sense that the volcano still simmered. 'All right, then. If that's the way you want it.' Cathy breathed a tremulous sigh of relief, which his next words turned into a gasp. 'But you're not leaving. I will.'

The only consolation, Cathy reflected as they drove back along the winding roads after dropping Adam off at the station, was that Rebecca knew nothing of her attempted 'escape'. She pulled up at the farmgate and watched the younger girl jump out to open it. At least their relationship was still untouched by the bitterness.

She parked the car and climbed down on to the cobbles. Behind the farmhouse, and all around, the fells rose smoothly against the soft brilliance of the sky. Cathy felt her eyes fill unexpectedly with tears: not of anger or self-pity, but of yearning for the beauty which nature had so casually poured over these hills and which she, in her preoccupation with her own problems, had almost ceased to notice. A picture of the little London office flashed into her mind. By comparison with the scene spread before her now it seemed like a prison cell, furnished with cardboard furniture.

A vision of Adam as she had seen him then overwhelmed her: Gulliver in Lilliput; a giant in the doll's house. He and this country were on the same scale—no wonder he had never been happy in London. She tried to imagine Mia Tannabrae against the backdrop of these fells, and failed. The actress's elfin beauty seemed somehow to demand a smaller, more delicate setting. Not necessarily urban, despite her jet-setting image, but more civilised, more controlled. A Cotswold cottage, perhaps.

And yet Becca seemed so much at home here, despite being physically her mother's double. She had an inner strength and determination which was very much her father's—that was something that Adam had had to recognise. Cathy found the thought comforting. Even though her interference had caused Rebecca so much pain at the time, perhaps her visit had served some useful purpose, something that would make up for the hurt that her defection was bound to cause.

'Cathy?'

She realised with a start that Rebecca was shaking her. Well, that was enough of that. She would just have to enjoy it while she could. Let Adam do what he had to and just wait for it all to blow over. Keep busy. Then she could go back to London and the agency and try to forget that the famous Nick Ballantyne had ever played the pirate with her emotions. She blinked the moisture from her eyes and ran through her mental list of tasks to be done.

'Of course I can manage.' Sally's confidence came through loud and clear over the long-distance line.

'And the Hoffmans will be delighted to keep Mrs MacIver. But what about you? Are you getting on all right? I would have thought you'd be sick of housework by now. That man certainly knows how to use his charm.'

And you don't know how true that is, Cathy thought bitterly as she outlined Adam's plan to her friend. But the evidence had been there from the first; it was her own fault that she had ignored it.

'It's his charm he's counting on—that's why I agreed to stay a bit longer.' She tried to ignore the sniff of disbelief which met her explanation. 'He thinks if he can talk to his ex-wife in person, instead of through solicitors, he may be able to bring her round. If he has to, he's going to offer her access on condition that she drops the custody claim. I'm sure it won't take too long now. So if you could hold the fort...'

'Well, of course, but you want to be careful, Cathy.' Sally sounded genuinely worried. 'He's taking advantage of you, in my opinion, and it sounds to me as if you might end up getting mixed up in some sordid court case.'

'He's paying very well, and the agency can't afford to turn up its nose at that sort of money.' The protest sounded false to her own ears, but her assistant seemed to take it at face-value.

'Yes...' There was an awkward pause. Then, 'Cathy, there's something I ought to tell you. I'm happy to look after things for as long as you like, but once you're back at the helm I'm going to start looking for another job.'

It was the last thing that Cathy had expected, and she hardly knew how to react. 'Oh—well, I shall miss you, of course——'

'But it's a relief, isn't it?' Cathy said nothing. It was, though she could hardly say so. But she didn't need to, for Sally went on, 'Since I've been doing the books, I've realised just what a drain on the agency my salary has been. I'm sorry, Cathy, I had no idea. It was wonderful of you to take me on when I left my job, and I'm very grateful, but it's time I moved on. You can manage on your own— and from the look of the bank account you can't afford not to. Dale's money is about all that balances the books at the moment, isn't it?'

'It certainly came at an opportune moment,' Cathy admitted ruefully. 'But you mustn't think you haven't been useful, Sally; you have. And I shall hate going back to working alone, but you're right about the economics. I was dreading having to talk to you about it; I know you didn't want to go back into publishing.'

'Oh, well, I'm not so sensitive now.' The philosophical tone couldn't entirely hide her feelings. 'I've put out a few feelers already; started going to all the right parties again. But working at Far Corners has certainly been an experience I wouldn't have missed—especially this last week on my own. If you ever decide to expand, I'd like to apply.'

'You've got it,' vowed Cathy. 'Oh, Sally, you don't know what a relief it is to know that I'm not going to have to make you redundant. I should have discussed it with you before, but——'

'You don't have to apologise. So, anyway, you can see that from my point of view you can stay away as long as you like. It's you I'm worried about.' She paused, and Cathy felt as if all her most private thoughts were being drawn down the phone line. Sally had always been far too astute where she was concerned. 'Cathy—is that all there is to it? You're not involved with him, are you?'

'No!' The denial came out with unexpected heat. 'No,' she repeated more calmly. 'It's just a favour. I feel sorry for his daughter mainly; she's a nice kid and you can imagine the sort of publicity a custody case would attract. Adam's hoping he can stop things from going that far. Anyway, how are things going down there? You must let me know what the response is like to those adverts.'

Cathy had the feeling that her assistant didn't wholly believe her, but she said nothing and the conversation passed to more practical matters until the end of the call.

She had picked up the phone absent-mindedly, expecting nothing more than Sally's latest report. Since she had been alone at the farm, her assistant had taken to phoning in daily. The sound of Adam's deep voice was like a physical shock. How long was it since she had heard from him? A week—ten days? There had been letters addressed to Becca, but nothing for her. She hadn't expected otherwise; after the way they had parted it had seemed that there was nothing left for them to say.

It was so unexpected that it took her a few minutes to concentrate on what he was saying. The tone sank in first: happy, excited. Not the harsh coldness of their last exchange. Then the words—and for a moment Cathy thought she must have missed some vital part of his message. It didn't seem to fit in. What was he saying?

'So there's a good chance that I might have got it all sorted out. Permanently. You don't know how grateful I am, Cathy—and how sorry I am for the way I've treated you. I used you, I know, but I was so terrified of losing Rebecca that I was blind to everything else. I'll make it up to you, I promise, if you'll let me, once all this is over.'

'But, Adam, what's happening?' Cathy felt herself being infected with his air of hope and excitement. It passed briefly through her mind that it was the first time since he had left that she had felt alive.

'I can't go into it all now; it may not come off. But I'm sure it will be all right, if she can just see Becca. Can you send her up today? There's a train at twelve thirty-five; I'll meet it if you think you could make it. She's done the trip before; just ask the guard to keep an eye on her when she has to change.'

'If who sees Becca? Mia?'

'Yes, of course. Is this a bad line? It's all down to you, Cathy. You told me that I was building her up in my mind as some kind of monster, and I was. No one could have been that bad. And I realise now that she must have had a lot to put up with from me to make her walk out the way she did. I've been seeing quite a lot of her these last few days, and once we stopped re-fighting old battles, we realised that we actually like each other. I'm sure that seeing Becca will clinch it. Make sure she brings that dress, will you? I can buy the rest down here. You were right; she needs some new stuff.'

Cathy couldn't find words to answer. What had happened in those few days to make such a radical difference? Mia must have decided not to press on with her claims—there was no other explanation. She felt a wave of desire for Adam's presence: to see the expression on his face, to touch him. The distorted telephone voice was his—and yet somehow wasn't him.

But his voice broke into her bewilderment with a touch of impatience. 'Look, it's really important that you get her on that train if you can. I'm sorry to spring it on you like this—I'll be coming back up in a day or two and I'll explain it all then.'

Cathy glanced at her watch. It was going to be touch and go. Adam was right; explanations would have to wait. 'OK, I think I can do it. Is there somewhere I can reach you if we miss it?' She scribbled down the number he gave her and said a hurried goodbye. She hadn't the faintest idea what was going on. And yet, hurrying out into the cobbled yard, she felt like singing.

They had made the station with only minutes to spare. Becca's face was bright with excitement and exertion on the other side of the thick glass as they waited for the train to pull away. Cathy could see her nervously fingering the small shoulder-bag which was her only luggage. It contained a change of underwear, pyjamas—and the dress, cleaned and pressed after its rescue from the ignominy of the waste-paper basket and restored to favour by Adam's request.

The train drew out and Cathy waved until it was out of sight, then walked back along the platform, tentatively probing her feelings as if testing with her tongue a tooth that might turn out to be painful. Just what did she feel? Since Adam had left for London she had deliberately stifled her emotions, trying not to think about the past or the future, trying not to visualise what her life would be like when she returned to London, and Becca and her father were no more than names in her computer's list of clients. But now...

She could no longer ignore the hopes that had been planted by that brief telephone conversation. If Adam had persuaded Mia to give up her claim then that meant he no longer had to marry...so if he still wanted her, she would know he was sincere.

Cathy smiled wryly at the paradox. When he had needed to marry her, she had felt forced to refuse; and yet now she knew without even considering it that she wanted to accept him—if she ever got another chance. She felt a moment of panic at the thought that she might not. How unreasonable had her behaviour really been? If Adam did love her, he must have found her lack of trust cruelly painful; no wonder his hot temper had got the better of him. She would just have to hope that he loved her enough to understand and forgive her stubborn resistance.

To spend the rest of her life here, with Adam ... The thought burned inside her, rekindling the glow she had thought was forever extinguished. And yet ... Could she really hand the agency over to Sally and become just another country housewife?

Yes, she told herself firmly. There was no other answer. It was futile to think of transplanting Far Corners to this remote place—it would be bankrupt within six months and both she and Sally would be out of a job. And a move down to London was out of the question. Even if she herself hadn't fallen under the spell of the lonely Dales country, she could never force Adam and Becca to give up the home they loved.

Driving home—yes, she had been right before, it *was* her home—Cathy had the sensation that she was growing lighter and lighter, as if her heart was a helium balloon swelling with happiness inside her. The windows were down and the sun-roof open and the warm wind that flowed round her shoulders seemed to be stripping away the worries and constraints of her old life.

She shook her head until the pins flew free, scattering over the leather upholstery and letting her hair stream freely backwards. She would miss the agency, of course. It was something that she had made; her baby. But she could keep in touch and there would be other things to claim her energies: Adam, of course, Becca, and perhaps other babies as well—the human kind.

'I could be pregnant already,' she whispered unsteadily to herself. And Adam, what would he feel
about that? She knew so little about him; suppose
he felt that after bringing up Rebecca he had done
his stint of parenthood? But, before the worry had
time to form and bite, the wind had whisked it away
with the others. She could hear Adam's voice reassuring her. 'There aren't any problems we can't
handle.' Why hadn't she realised before how true
that was?

When she untied the gate and swung it back, the
simple action was suddenly charged with sym-
bolism. Leaving the car, she ran forward on to the
cobbles and flung out her arms in sudden joy. 'I
love him!' she shouted, and laughed at the hens'
flustered reactions to this unheard-of behaviour.
'I'm home!'

The rest of the day was touched with the same
magic. Feeding the animals, milking, tidying the
house: everything had taken on a new feeling of
permanency, of belonging. It must be like this, she
thought, to own a beautiful painting instead of just
looking at it in an art gallery. There was pleasure
in touching the worn wood of the heavy furniture
and in walking barefoot on the cool stone floors.
The silky touch of the banisters as she made her
way up to bed was like a caress. And, as soon as
she lay down, she knew that she would never sleep.

With the intention of finding something to read,
she slipped down the moonlit corridor to Adam's
room and switched on the light. The room, always
stark, looked unnaturally tidy and unlived-in, and

yet somehow gave off an overwhelmingly strong sensation of his presence. Cathy stood immobile as the memories flooded over her. She closed her eyes and he was there with her, his arms around her, pulling her to him as their lips met and fused, mutually caressing, teasing, intoxicating. She could feel his body pressing against hers, feel the firmness of his chest and legs through the thin fabric of her nightdress. It was so real that when she opened her eyes she felt dazed and lost to find herself alone.

On impulse she went over to the tall chest of drawers and pulled open a drawer at random. The scent of him seemed to flood her heightened senses and she pulled out the rough woollen jersey that lay on top. It was the one he had worn the night he had rescued her on the moor, and she buried her face in the Aran knit, breathing in the warm, musky smell and remembering the feel of his strong hands caressing her and of the weight of his body crushing the harsh wool against her skin.

Moved by an overwhelming need for his closeness, she pulled off her nightdress and threw it on to the chair by the bed. Reaching over her head to pull the jersey on in its place, she caught sight of herself in the long mirror. Her long hair curled richly around her naked shoulders and pale breasts, and Cathy felt a surge of exultation. He would see her like this; they would come together as they had done on the moor. She would feel his weight on her again and the hardness of his body against her. Pulling the jersey tightly round her, she went over to Adam's bed. The sheets were cool and fresh and impersonal as she slipped between them, but somehow his presence still lurked. She had only to close her eyes and abandon herself to the dream.

CHAPTER ELEVEN

THE FORMING butter made a satisfactory flip-flop sound in the little wooden churn which she had rescued from the attic. It was coming. Not too much longer now, or it would turn greasy, especially in this heat. That was it. Now to wash it out. She ran the buttermilk off and carried it over to the fridge, taking a surreptitious drink from the jug before she shut the door, and wiping her mouth as guiltily as she had ever done at home in her mother's kitchen. The cool, sour liquid was deliciously refreshing.

What a shame she hadn't thought of resurrecting the old churn while Rebecca was at home; it would have made a good project to keep the blues at bay. But then, according to her mother, only a happy woman could make good butter, so perhaps it wouldn't have been a good idea. By that token, this ought to be the best she had ever made.

She was on her third change of rinsing water when the telephone rang for the first time. The butter was forgotten as she rushed to answer it, only to hear an unknown woman's strident tones instead of the rich masculinity of the voice she had been hoping for.

'I'm afraid that Mr Dale is away from home at the moment,' she said politely, trying to keep the disappointment from her voice. How ridiculous to behave like a lovesick schoolgirl. 'This is his house-keeper speaking. Can I help you?'

'Oh, yes, Miss ... er ...'

'Aylward,' Cathy supplied, ignoring what seemed to be a rather hostile tone. 'Can I take a message for Mr Dale?'

'Miss Aylward, yes. This is Miss Anstruther, Rebecca Dale's class teacher. Indeed you can take a message, or perhaps you can help me yourself. Why is Rebecca not at school? Is she unwell?'

'At school? But surely term doesn't start until next week?'

'On the contrary, Miss Aylward, it started on Monday. The autumn term is particularly important. Ground lost at the beginning of a course is very difficult to regain, even for the most hard-working of pupils.' The implication was clearly that Rebecca did not fall into this category. 'Notice of the dates of the new terms was given very clearly in my end-of-term letter to parents. So I take it that Rebecca will be at school this afternoon?'

For one wild moment, Cathy was tempted to tell this pompous woman exactly what she thought of her, but she restrained the impulse. It would do Becca no good to antagonise her teacher any further. 'I'm afraid that won't be possible, Miss Anstruther; you see, Mr Dale has taken her with him to London. He was under the impression that she had another week's holiday. I will have to contact him and arrange for her to come back.'

But not before Adam is ready for her to leave, she added in silent rebellion. Nothing you could teach her could possibly be as important as what she is learning at the moment. 'It may take a day or two to get hold of him,' she went on, preparing the way. 'Their plans weren't fixed. But I will leave messages for him.'

'I see. Well, that will have to do. Perhaps you could inform Mr Dale that I would like to speak to him on his return. This is not the first time he has shown a blatant disregard for the school time-table. I would like to point out that under the Education Act of...'

'I'm sure this was a genuine mistake, Miss Anstruther,' Cathy soothed—unsuccessfully, to judge from the sniff which was the teacher's only reply. 'But I'll get in touch with him as soon as I can. Thank you for ringing.'

She replaced the phone with relief, only for it to ring again almost under her hand. Again she felt her heart hammering in anticipation. This time, surely it must be Adam. But when she picked it up, it was to hear Sally's cheerful voice.

'Hello, Cathy, how are things going up there?' Behind the casual enquiry, Cathy could sense her friend's real concern. If only she could tell her the good news—but better not until she had heard from Adam that Mia's agreement was signed and sealed.

'Oh, fine. You don't need to worry about me, Sally. In fact I'm more or less on holiday at the moment because Adam has taken Becca down to London for a few days. I'm living a life of ease.'

'Really? That sounds like providence—as a matter of fact I was going to make a suggestion but

I wasn't sure how the great man would react to you taking time off. I rather had the impression that he owned you body and soul—or thought he did.'

Cathy smiled at her friend's caustic comments. 'Honestly, Sally, he's not that bad. But what was this suggestion?'

'Well, now that the adverts have been in for a couple of weeks, we've had quite a few replies. In fact, I've already interviewed some of the most hopeful-sounding. But there were five from up your way or further: Yorkshire, Northumberland and two from Scotland. And when I totted up the cost of their interview expenses it came to a terrifying figure.

'Well, I know how you feel about employing staff we haven't seen, but I was wondering if we could make do with a phone interview—no, I know, but the bank account is nearly bare until your next cheque arrives and we can't afford to turn staff away.

'Anyway, then I had a brainwave. If you could take a day off and borrow Adam's car, you could meet them in Newcastle. It would cut the fares down to less than half; and they could all do it as a day trip. It would save us a fortune. I don't see how he could object, really, especially if he's not there. What do you think?'

'I think you're brilliant, Sally. I've always had to turn down a lot of the northern applicants before; it just wasn't worth the expense unless they sounded too good to miss. You're wasted as a secretary; I should have got you involved in running the agency before.'

'Oh, well, it was just because you were on the spot. It wouldn't have been worth it before, with your fare and time to take into consideration, I don't suppose. But now the agency has a temporary northern branch...'

Sally's words seemed to jog something loose in her brain, and Cathy could hardly suppress her excitement at the idea which began to develop. 'Look, are you any closer to finding another job yet?'

'Well, yes and no. I've heard through the grapevine that—oh, just a moment, Cathy. If you're thinking of suggesting that I should head off into the middle of nowhere when you come back and start a Far Corners Arctic division, thanks, but no, thanks. I've enjoyed my spell of power, but I'm not prepared to pursue it that far! You don't need to worry about me; I'll get something fixed up.'

Cathy hugged her inspiration close as she reassured her friend. 'Don't worry, I wouldn't dream of suggesting it. I know what a London sparrow you are. But don't rush into arranging anything else just at the moment, will you? I might just have an idea.'

More than an idea—a revelation, the answer to all her lingering doubts. Cathy wondered why it had never occurred to her before, but then, she had become so used to thinking of expansion as the cause of the agency's problems that it took a touch of lateral thinking to realise that it might also be their salvation. To employ two people to cope with the same amount of business as one had been economic stupidity; but if the second person could actually generate new business...

With her mind distracted, she drained the last of the washing water from the churn and scooped the creamy mass out on to a board. It was worth trying, at least. She turned the plan over and over as she worked the cool yellow butter, and it all seemed to hang together. Sally could take care of the London office while she herself started up a northern branch in much the same way that she had originally founded the agency: working from home.

Home. Cathy found herself momentarily distracted by a superstitious feeling that she was 'counting her chickens'. It was that word again; she had stopped trying to fight it. But this was home now, and if that was tempting fate there wasn't much she could do about it. Mentally she shrugged her shoulders and turned back to the problem in hand.

If her idea worked, the agency would gain by attracting all the northern clients who might never think of contacting a London-based agency, and all the staff whom it had previously been uneconomic to interview. All without losing the advantages of a London base.

And, if it failed, she would be in no worse a position. She could just bow out and leave the running of the agency to Sally as she had planned. But the more she let the idea take root, the more convinced she was that it could succeed. Perhaps eventually she might even open a proper office somewhere like

Kendal or Richmond? Then if she could take on someone else to run it—she pulled up, laughing at herself, realising that she was running much too far ahead. The time for empire-building would be when she had proved that the idea was sound; but it was an exciting thought.

And a sobering one, in a way. She knew that her present delight was an indication of just how much she would miss the agency if she did have to give it up. That she would do it, if she had to, was no longer in doubt. The prospect of losing Adam altogether had rearranged her priorities for good. But how much better if she could have both.

With a feeling of satisfaction and accomplishment, Cathy shaped the butter into a neat block and carefully wrapped it in paper. Next time, Becca could help her; she would enjoy that. The thought reminded Cathy of the earlier phone call. She was tempted to ignore it and pretend that she hadn't been able to reach them with the news. After all, what did it really matter if Rebecca missed another few days of school? What could she possibly learn from that old dragon, anyway? But then if by some terrible chance Adam had failed to reach agreement with Mia, it might cause him more problems. Cathy remembered the ominous mention of Education Acts ...

And besides, she couldn't suppress a selfish hope that it might speed their return. She hunted out her scribbled note of the number Adam had given her and began to dial. A woman's voice answered: smooth, efficient and with a slight American accent.

'This is Miss Tannabrae's secretary. Can I help you?'

Cathy felt flustered; somehow she had expected the number to be that of a hotel, and she suddenly realised that she didn't know which name Adam would be using. 'Good morning,' she started uncertainly. 'I was given this number to contact Mr—um—Dale. This is his housekeeper speaking.'

Nick Ballantyne hadn't existed when he knew Mia before; surely he would be using his own name? It seemed that she was right. The efficient American knew all about Mr Dale.

'I'm sorry, I'm afraid he and Miss Tannabrae are out right now, looking at houses. They didn't expect to return until late; I know that Mr Dale was anxious to make a final decision today and they had a number of properties to see. But I have the estate agent's number if the message is urgent.'

Cathy was half-way through her explanation before the implications started to sink in. She remembered reading somewhere that the victim of a stab wound initially feels nothing more than a blow: no searing pain, no sensation of being cut. Afterwards, she thought that something like that must have happened to her, some activation of a natural buffer against sudden pain. Or how could she have continued the conversation as normally as she did, when every word only confirmed how completely she had misread the situation?

'So if you could ask him to let me know when Rebecca will be coming back? He did say it would be any day...' Cathy's voice tailed out.

'Well, I will communicate with Mr Dale, of course, but I think I can tell you his plans. He's planning to drive up tomorrow and collect the rest of Rebecca's things; I guess you'd better tell her teacher that she won't be back for a while. I know Miss Tannabrae was arranging for her to join the school on the set for a few weeks. She thought it would be interesting for the girl.'

'On the set?' Cathy felt as if she had been handed the pieces to a jigsaw which contained some vital information and was struggling to sort them out.

'The film set. Miss Tannabrae starts filming again next week. She and Mr Dale thought it would be nice for Rebecca to join them, and take lessons with the juvenile actors. I guess they just want to be together at the moment.'

'Yes, I suppose so.' Why was her mind working so slowly? She had to ask the right questions. She had to know how far things had gone. 'Did you say Mr Dale would be driving up? But he hasn't taken his car; it's still here at the farm.'

'Well, I guess they are planning to use Miss Tannabrae's automobile.' Cathy could tell that the woman thought she was asking unnecessary questions. To the secretary she was just a housekeeper making a fuss.

'I'd like to know what arrangements to make,' she said, trying to keep the desperation out of her voice. 'So I need to know when they are arriving and for how long. Will Miss Tannabrae be coming up, too?'

'Yes, that's right. They will be there for lunch at about one. And Mr Dale said there would be no need to ask you to prepare the spare room.'

'So they will be leaving again that day?' Cathy persisted. The alternative—that they might share his room—was too terrible to contemplate.

'I guess so.' The secretary sounded uninterested. 'I don't believe he said exactly. Is there a problem?'

'No, no problem. Thank you. I'll expect them.'

'Have a nice day, now.'

The irony of those parting words seemed to penetrate the protective layer of confusion that had surrounded her, and suddenly Cathy knew quite clearly just how wrong she had been. She must have misinterpreted Adam's words totally. What had he said? She racked her brain for the words, but she hardly remembered them. It was the tone she remembered: happy, relieved, excited. He had said that he was making arrangements that would solve the problem permanently, that he had found that he and Mia actually liked each other. And she had assumed that he meant that he had persuaded Mia to relinquish her claim. But he hadn't said that. And what he had meant was something radically different.

Instead of fighting Mia, he had found that he still loved her—and she must have felt the same. He was even prepared to move down to London to be with Mia, something that Cathy knew he would never have done for her. And, after all his determination to keep Becca away from her mother's showbusiness life, now he was letting her be plunged into the thick of it.

It couldn't be true! Cathy's mind ran wildly through other explanations, but inside she knew the truth. She could remember so clearly his joy on the telephone; that had been the voice of a man in love. She had thought it was for herself; why else had she read so much into that short call? But it had been for Mia, his fairy woman. His seal wife had come back to him, and he didn't intend to lose her again. Hence the hurry to bring Rebecca down and to buy a London house. He wouldn't make the same mistake twice.

No doubt he would keep the farm for weekends and holidays, she thought bitterly. He might even arrange with Hallgarth to keep Minty for Becca to ride when they came up. Mia would talk to her friends about their sweet little country cottage and invent excuses for going there as infrequently as possible. She would probably plant flowers in the butter churn that Cathy had so carefully scrubbed clean. There would be no other use for it. No one could keep a cow at a weekend retreat.

She had felt for the agony of the wife of mortal kind when her husband went down to the sea to stare at the waves and sigh. Cathy realised now that she should have wondered what would have happened if the seal wife ever returned. Was there any doubt that he would have taken her back? And the fairy kind were not noted for their tact or gentleness. It would not occur to her to stay away.

What should she do? She could go, of course. There was nothing to stop her driving to the station and leaving on the next train to London. She could show Adam that he didn't 'own her body and soul', as Sally had put it. He had no right to expect her to stay; now that there was no longer any problem about Becca, their agreement was at an end.

But as she sat there at the kitchen table, with the unshed tears burning at her eyelids, she knew that she wasn't going to leave. Why not, she wasn't sure. Partly it was a desire to face them out, to get through the visit without comment or reaction. Partly a feeling that, if she left now, she would be running away. And partly, she was honest enough to admit, it was a morbid sort of curiosity; a desire to see this woman who could bewitch millions from a cinema screen, or one man and a child.

But mostly it was the feeling that the story needed an ending and that only by staying would she find it. If she ran away, she might be spared some pain, but the ache would go on and on. She had to see them for herself, or there would be hope. She had to kill that hope. And she wanted to say goodbye to Rebecca.

CHAPTER TWELVE

HER face set, Cathy smoothed the last escaping tendril of hair into place and skewered it viciously with a hairpin. Then she tentatively shook her head. Nothing came loose. Well, she would do. Cold water had removed most traces of her sleepless night, leaving just a slight redness around the eyes which could have been due to hay-fever or a summer cold. She wasn't beautiful, but then she didn't need to be. After all, she was only the housekeeper.

She glanced at her watch. Only another half-hour to go. Everything was ready: a lunch of cold chicken and salad laid out in the dining-room, a bottle of white wine in the fridge, home-made rolls cooling on a wire rack in the kitchen. Somehow Cathy had found a perverse kind of pleasure in her meticulous preparations for Mia's visit. To the actress she would be nothing more than a servant—well, then, she would be a bloody good one. And perhaps, by concentrating on her role, the visit might be easier to bear.

Unable to settle, she went to check round the rooms one final time. There was Rebecca's, unnaturally tidy, with a suitcase containing all her treasures lying ready on the bed. The bed where she had drunk champagne and orange juice in the middle of the night, where her legs had brushed against his under the covers; the bed where she had fallen in love. The tears prickled her eyes warningly and she hastily shut the door.

Then Adam's room. She had hoovered and polished it until it shone, but still there was that lingering sense of his presence which had so intoxicated her the night before last. The Aran jersey was in the wash, but the warm scent of him still hung on the air—or was it just her imagination? But she knew that if she closed her eyes he would be there again, pressing against her, urgent and passionate in his loving. Keeping them firmly open, she backed out into the hallway. That was why she was still here; why she was waiting for him. She had to lay that ghost.

And then they were arriving. Cathy heard the car pull up and turned away from the window for a last look around the kitchen, to say goodbye. After this, it wouldn't be hers any longer; it would belong to Mia, who probably didn't want it at all. It was going to be very difficult not to hate her.

But, in the event, it wasn't difficult at all. There was a commotion at the door which brought old Betsy limping from her place in the sun to greet the visitors, and then Becca exploded into the room, dragging by the hand a woman who could have been her older sister. Cathy hadn't been prepared for the actress's shy fragility, nor for the warmth of her smile and her welcome. It was impossible not to respond, especially with Becca performing the introductions.

'Guess who this is, Cathy!' she burst out, her face glowing with pleasure.

Cathy glanced up at Mia and their eyes met. Cathy recognised in the other woman the same fondness that Becca stirred in her, and felt an icicle melt from her heart. She loved Becca, at least. And Becca was obviously completely absorbed in her.

'I'm not sure I know,' she answered solemnly. 'Perhaps you had better introduce us.'

'This is my mother! My real, true mother. And she's a famous actress, aren't you, Mummy? That's why she couldn't live with us like other people's mothers. But now I'm old enough, Daddy says I can go and see her making films and I can have lessons with the children who are in the film. And Mummy says that if I'm good and if the director says I can, I might be able to be in the film as well.'

The two women shook hands. 'I'm afraid she's rather over-excited at the moment,' the actress said, with a touch of embarrassment. 'But after a couple of weeks she'll realise that it's all rather boring, really. Just a lot of waiting about and doing things over and over again. But we thought it would be as well for her to see it.'

That 'we' hurt, but Cathy couldn't blame the speaker. How should she know what pain she was causing? Adam would hardly have boasted of their relationship. Before she could reply, Becca was off at top speed again.

'How's Minty? Did you remember not to give him any oats while I wasn't here?' She turned to her mother. 'You mustn't give ponies oats if you're not riding them, or they get fat and they might get ill.' Then, to Cathy, 'Minty's going to come and live with us in London. He's going to go all the way in a horse-box and we're going to take Bonnie, too.'

'Becca!' Mia protested helplessly. 'You know Daddy asked you not to mention that. I'm sorry, Cathy—you don't mind me calling you Cathy, do you? Only, with Becca and Adam calling you that, it's how I think of you. I'm sorry, I know Adam wanted to talk to you himself first. Oh, Becca, what a chatterbox you are!'

The child looked so stricken that Cathy almost forgot her own pain. 'Don't worry, darling. We'll pretend I didn't hear and then Daddy can tell me.' She walked into the kitchen and sat down, followed by the other two. 'Where is Adam, anyway?'

'Oh, he's looking at my car; I'm afraid it's not very practical for these roads. We went over a rock about half a mile back and he thinks it might have done something to the exhaust.'

As if prompted by her words, Adam appeared in the doorway, wiping his hands on a piece of rag. Cathy's heart lurched and she knew at once that staying had been a mistake. She was glad to have met Mia and to know that Becca would be happy, but to see Adam and know that she had lost him was sheer torture. Every line on his face, every curl of tawny hair, was suddenly infinitely dear. She had thought that she remembered him so vividly; the look and the touch and the sound of him; and yet to see him again made her memories seem like faded snapshots.

Then he looked directly at her, his face alive with a happiness that wasn't for her, and she thought for a moment that she was going to faint. Jumping up, she forced her face into a smile. 'I've set lunch out in the dining-room, if you're ready to eat. Becca, why don't you show your mother where she can wash her hands?' They left the room and Cathy hurried after them. Adam was scrubbing the oil off his skin over the kitchen sink and she had no intention of risking a tête-à-tête with him until she had recovered her composure. She had given up all hope of laying her ghosts. Now her only desire was to survive the rest of their visit with some sort of self-control.

For most of the meal the conversation was mercifully general. Mia, although at first reluctant to talk about herself, told some amusing stories about her life in films. Becca demanded a blow-by-blow account of everything that had happened on the farm while she had been away, and was most impressed to discover that the butter she was eating had been made from Bonnie's creamy milk. Adam said very little, merely watching, and smiling his satisfaction.

All happy families, thought Cathy bitterly. He's so pleased with himself that he can't see what it's doing to me. But perhaps that was for the best; his pity would have been more than she could bear.

There was only one difficult moment, at the end of the meal. Becca had been excused to go and say hello to her pony while Adam and Cathy finished their wine and Mia sipped her mineral water. As if she had been waiting for a chance to speak, Mia leaned over to Cathy as soon as the child left the room.

'I can't tell you how grateful we both are for everything you've done, Cathy. If it hadn't been for you, we'd still have been snarling at each other through solicitors, and poor little Becca would have ended up being torn apart. I don't know how you managed to stay with this terrible man long enough to talk sense into him, but I'm very glad you did.'

Cathy felt herself reddening and her eyes start to fill. Pushing her chair back from the table, she mumbled something about coffee and rushed out to the kitchen. No one followed her, and by the time the coffee had dripped through the filter she was back in control. To her immense relief, when she returned to the dining-room, Mia was preparing to go.

'I'm sorry to be rushing off like this, but they've brought my filming schedule forward and I have to be on the set at six tomorrow morning. And Adam thinks I should pop into Rebecca's school on the way and explain what's happening. He seems to think it will come better from me.'

Adam grinned, an expression of such casual intimacy that it tore at Cathy's heart. 'I'd love to see that old bat's face when she sees you,' he said. 'Thriller writers may not cut much ice with her, but I rather think ravishingly beautiful, world-famous actresses are different. You'll have her eating out of your hand, and why not? Everyone else does.'

Including you, thought Cathy sadly, as they waved goodbye to Mia and her daughter in the incongruous little sports car. And now comes the difficult bit. What will he do? Hand over my paycheque and drive me to the station? Insist on an emotional farewell scene? Or invite me to the wedding?

Adam stood, looking after the car, until the last notes of the engine had died away. Then he turned back to Cathy. 'She's a very lovable person, isn't he?'

She forced herself to reply. 'Yes. And she's very fond of Becca. They make a lovely pair.'

'Yes.' There was a long pause. 'You don't mind about Becca going with her, do you? We thought it was the best thing.'

Cathy shook her head and looked at the ground, no longer daring to trust her voice. Adam didn't appear to notice. He seemed to be trying to find the right words, scuffing the cobbles with his foot in a way that reminded Cathy poignantly of his daughter.

At last, the words seemed to burst out of him. 'You were right all along; I'd built her up in my mind into a mixture of angel and devil. I wasn't rational where she was concerned. It wasn't until you more or less forced me to do something drastic that I went to see her—and discovered she was just a woman who'd had a lot to bear, and had been forced to make a very difficult choice. We had to

get to know each other all over again. It was
mistake having kept Becca apart from her all thi
time; they both got things out of proportion. W
could so easily have ended up destroying eac
other.'

Cathy was silent. What did he expect from her
Her blessing? Absolution? The price of his hap
piness had been the destruction of her own. Didn
he realise that? But he was still talking, the word
pouring out. Suddenly he swung round to face he
directly and seized her hands in his.

'I'm not going to make the same mistake agair
Cathy. I've had to realise what a mess I made c
my marriage last time, and I've sorted out m
priorities. This time, some of the sacrifices are goin
to be on my side.' He took a deep breath. 'I'r
moving down to London—or near Londor
anyway. There are plenty of places in the Hom
Counties where you can buy space and privacy i
you have enough money. We'll be able to take Mint
and Bonnie with us, and keep this place for ho
idays and weekends.' He stopped, obviously waitin
for some reaction. 'Well?'

Oh, God, prayed Cathy, just let me last anothe
ten minutes. Let me get through this withou
breaking down. She took a deep breath and sai
shakily, 'I hope you'll be happy there. I'm glad yo
can take Minty and Bonnie. Becca would be upse
to lose them.'

'I can be happy anywhere, so long as you'r
happy. I know how much the agency means to you

For a moment the world seemed to spin round, nd the next thing Cathy knew, Adam had scooped er up and was carrying her back into the house. Ie pulled out a kitchen chair and sat down with er on his lap, pulling her close to him and holding er tight. Cathy didn't dare to move or speak for ear of extinguishing the tiny spark of hope his rords had kindled.

'Say you'll come with me, Cathy. Say you'll aarry me. You've seen Mia; there's no problem aere now. Look, I've been going round the estate gents already; Mia's been helping me.' He pro-uced a bundle of estate agents' hand-outs from is back pocket. 'These are the ones that Becca and I liked best, but it's all up to you. I can't tell if ou're pleased or not, Cathy. Please say yes.'

At last Cathy's voice managed to force itself past 1e lump of joy in her throat. 'Oh, Adam!' She lung to him as she had in her terror on the moor, acked by sobbing, trying to gulp out an expla-ation as she wept with relief and happiness. 'I 1ought ... I thought that you and Mia ...' Adam 1st held her, gently stroking her back until the orm subsided.

'Oh, my poor darling love. I'm so sorry. I should ave explained—I was so full of it myself that it ever occurred to me that you didn't know what as going on. Mia and I are friends now, and we've greed that she'll see a lot more of Becca in future, ut there's nothing else. It's you I want to marry, athy. And Becca needs you as well; at the moment, lia is enchanted by her, but in six months the

novelty will have worn off for both of them. W
both need you, Cathy. You'll say yes, won't you?

He took her hand in his, and she felt somethin
cool and hard slide on to her finger. 'I'd begun t
think I'd never see you wear it,' he murmured. 'Bu
now it's on, it's staying. Even if I have to have
welded in place.'

Cathy could hardly bring herself to look dowr
scarcely daring to trust the happiness which ha
betrayed her before. But, when she did, the flam
inside her flared and burned as brightly as the rubie
which lay like drops of heart's blood against th
pallor of her skin. And she knew that, this time
there would be no disillusion.

The last day and night were already receding int
the distance, like a bad dream on waking. Adam'
arms were round her and the chill which had crep
over her was being replaced by a suffusing warmtl
Adam loved her; he loved her enough to give u
the home he adored. He was crushing her to him
the gentle strength of his arms squeezing her a
though their bodies could merge into one. It wa
going to be all right.

'Cathy, answer me. I've got to know you're mine
You will come down to London with us, won
you?'

'No, Adam, I can't.' She turned her face awa
to hide the gleam of mischief in her wet eyes.

His grip tightened until it was nearly painfu
'What the——? Why the hell not? You love m
don't you? I won't believe you if you say you don'
anyway. So what damn stupid excuse are you goin

to come up with this time? What do you want from me, for God's sake—blood?'

'It's no use, Adam. It's my job, I can't give it up.'

'No one's asking you to give up your job, you idiot woman. That's the whole point of moving down south. Are you quite all right, or has happiness addled your brain?'

'But, Adam—I don't work in London any more. Didn't I mention it? I'm opening a new northern branch of the agency; in fact, I was just looking for some suitable premises. You don't know of anyone with a room to spare in an old farmhouse or something, do you? At a reasonable rent?'

The slowly dawning understanding on his face was too much for Cathy. She collapsed into giggles.

'Why you little... Do you mean what I think you mean? Are you sure, Cathy? I know how much the agency means to you.'

'I'm sure. Nothing could make me leave this place now, Adam. And I could never take you and Becca away. We belong here, all of us.'

He stared at her almost unbelievingly for a moment. Their faces were so close that she could feel the warmth radiating from his skin and feel the moisture of his breath. Then he was moving, coming closer, and her lips parted in welcome. With infinite delicacy, he kissed first her lower and then her upper lip, teasing them gently with his tongue until Cathy felt her mouth aflame, her lips swollen with desire.

As if restraint was an art, they tasted each other's lips, sipping the cup of pleasure that both knew was full to overflowing. His hand brushed the down on her cheek with a feather's touch, tracing a cobweb of electric anticipation across her skin. Her hands moved lightly over his strong body, touching, caressing, testing incredulously the solidity, the reality, of his presence.

'What an unreasonable woman you are.'

'Me?'

'Of course. There I am, being noble and sacrificing myself for you, and you calmly turn round and give me everything I ever wanted. I call that unreasonable.'

'Well, I had a good teacher. You're the most unreasonable man I've ever met. You bulldoze me into coming here; you bulldoze me into staying; you even threaten to sue me if I leave!'

He had the grace to look embarrassed. 'I'm sorry about that, Cathy, but I was desperate. I think I would have tied you to the bed if necessary. I was sure that if I could just keep you at the farm, then sooner or later you'd come round, whereas if you left... I was terrified that you might drift out of my life completely. I thought if I could demolish all your excuses, you'd have no choice but to give in.'

'Bulldozing again!'

'Well, it worked, didn't it? If I'd left things to you, you'd still be in London sending unsuitable housekeepers to long-suffering clients and my book would have been even later than it's going to be anyway. I told you before, some people just need bulldozing.' As if to demonstrate, he pulled her towards him again and stifled her words with his mouth, sliding his hand under her shirt and capturing one breast in his rough palm.

Cathy felt a sense of her own powerlessness; she had let him inside her guard and now she was utterly defenceless against him. And yet she knew that never before had she been so safe. 'You're nothing but a pirate. I hope you're not planning to bully me like this when we're married.'

'Of course I am. Why abandon a winning streak? For a start, if I ever catch you wearing a hairpin again, I intend to beat you.'

'But they're practical——' she protested teasingly.

'I don't care. I've never actually seen a male hedgehog after a night of passion, but I don't suppose it's a pretty sight. You've already blacked my eye for me; I don't plan to let you put it out altogether.'

'I could just take them out when we go to bed.'

'In that case, you'd better start now.' Jumping to his feet, he dragged her out of the kitchen, holding her hands in one hand and with the other tugging the hairpins from her hair, regardless of her squeals of discomfort.

'Upstairs, woman!' Breathless with laughter and mounting excitement, Cathy found herself being half chased, half carried to his room and dumped unceremoniously on the bed.

'And I'm warning you——' he was unbuckling his belt, and Cathy couldn't take her eyes off his hands '—you're not leaving this bed until you agree to all my unreasonable demands.'

'I'm a stubborn woman,' she said wickedly, watching the denim wrinkle down over his hips. 'It could take weeks.'

'That sounds just fine to me. I can think of ways to pass the time. Like playing "I-Feel".'

And, as he began to demonstrate, she had to admit that he was right.

Harlequin Presents·

Coming Next Month

#1287 BELONGING Sally Cook
Mandy always knew she was adopted, but having grown up so different from
her adoptive parents, she decides to trace her real mother. While her search is
successful, she finds the attractive Grant Livingstone is highly suspicious of
her motives.

#1288 THE ULTIMATE CHOICE Emma Darcy
According to Kelly, the new owner of Marian Park is an arrogant swine who
betrayed her grandfather and who wants to ruin Kelly's show-jumping career.
Determined not to be stopped, she confronts Justin St. John, with all
guns blazing....

#1289 TAKING CHANCES Vanessa Grant
It seems an odd request even for Misty's detective agency. Why does
Zeb Turner want her to kidnap him? Finding out, Misty lands herself with more
than she'd bargained for—maybe even more than she can cope with!

#1290 RUNAWAY WIFE Charlotte Lamb
Francesca has everything, so it seems—Oliver, her handsome, successful
husband; a healthy son; and a lovely home. She believes she's merely a symbol
of his success to Oliver and needs—and wants—far more than that from life.

#1291 THE SEDUCTION OF SARA Joanna Mansell
Sara isn't too pleased to have Lucas Farraday following her around Peru. She
thinks he's just a penniless drifter. Gradually she relaxes and gets used to his
presence and his help. And that's when Lucas makes his next move....

#1292 RECKLESS HEART Kate Proctor
Ever since Sian McAllister's new boss, Nicholas Sinclair, had jumped to the
wrong conclusions about her, life has been difficult. And the situation
becomes impossible when Sian realizes that despite their strong
disagreements, she's falling in love with him.

#1293 GENTLE DECEPTION Frances Roding
Rosy's love for her married cousin, Elliott, is entirely platonic, but not everyone
sees it that way. To prove them wrong, Rosy has to find herself a man.
Callum Blake is perfectly willing to be her pretend lover—yet what if pretence
becomes reality?

#1294 DESIGNED WITH LOVE Kathryn Ross
Drew Sheldon is Amanda's ex-fiancé—and when her father sells the family firm
to him, Amanda has a problem. She needs her job, but can she live with the
power Drew now holds over her when she has an idea he really might
want revenge?

Available in August wherever paperback books are sold, or through
Harlequin Reader Service:

In the U.S.
901 Fuhrmann Blvd.
P.O. Box 1397
Buffalo, N.Y. 14240-1397

In Canada
P.O. Box 603
Fort Erie, Ontario
L2A 5X3

HARLEQUIN
American Romance

THE LOVES OF A CENTURY...

Join American Romance in a nostalgic look back at the Twentieth Century—at the lives and loves of American men and women from the turn-of-the-century to the dawn of the year 2000.

Journey through the decades from the dance halls of the 1900s to the discos of the seventies ... from Glenn Miller to the Beatles ... from Valentino to Newman ... from corset to miniskirt ... from beau to Significant Other.

Relive the moments ... recapture the memories.

Look now for the CENTURY OF AMERICAN ROMANCE series in Harlequin American Romance. In one of the four American Romance titles appearing each month, for the next twelve months, we'll take you back to a decade of the Twentieth Century, where you'll relive the years and rekindle the romance of days gone by.

Don't miss a day of the CENTURY OF AMERICAN ROMANCE.

A CENTURY OF
AMERICAN ROMANCE
1900's

The women...the men...the passions...
the memories....

CAR-1

Take 4 bestselling love stories FREE

Plus get a FREE surprise gift!

Harlequin Superromance®

A powerful restaurant conglomerate that draws the
best and brightest to its executive ranks. Now almost
eighty years old, Vanessa Hamilton, the founder of
Hamilton House, must choose a successor.
Who will it be?

Matt Logan: He's always been the company man, the
quintessential team player. But tragedy in his
daughter's life and a passionate love affair made him
make some hard choices....

Paula Steele: Thoroughly accomplished, with a sharp
mind, perfect breeding and looks to die for, Paula
thrives on challenges and wants to have it all ...
but is this right for her?

Grady O'Connor: Working for Hamilton House was
his salvation after Vietnam. The war had messed him
up but good and had killed his storybook marriage.
He's been given a second chance—only he doesn't
know what the hell he's supposed to do with it....

Harlequin Superromance invites you to enjoy Barbara
Kaye's dramatic and emotionally resonant miniseries
about mature men and women making life-changing
decisions. Don't miss:

- CHOICE OF A LIFETIME—a July 1990 release.
- CHALLENGE OF A LIFETIME
  —a December 1990 release.
- CHANCE OF A LIFETIME—an April 1991 release.